THE BLOOD OF CARTERVILLE

THE BLOOD OF CARTERVILLE

A CARTERVILLE MYSTERY

ROBERT J. MCCARTER

LITTLE HUMMINGBIRD PUBLISHING

CARTERVILLE MYSTERIES

Each Carterville Mystery is stand-alone, but things do change in Carterville. The chronological order of the books are:

- **Out of a Christmas Sky**
- **Destroyer of Carterville**
- **The Blood of Carterville**

Note: The events of this story take place a little over a year after *Destroyer of Carterville*.

INTRODUCTION TO THE SECOND EDITION

Something unusual happened with these Carterville books. This was the first book I wrote and I knew I wanted more Carterville, but I was so fascinated with the conflict that came to a head in this book, that I had to go back in time and explore how things got to this point.

So I wrote two other novels, *Out of a Christmas Sky* and *Destroyer of Carterville,* to explore that history. In that process I got to know the layout of the town and its characters and conflicts much better. This has necessitated some revisions to this story.

The plot is exactly the same, but the manuscript has been updated to reflect my better understanding of Carterville and its characters. There are small changes throughout, and only Chapter 5 is new.

I hope you enjoy reading about this strange little mountain town as much as I have enjoyed writing about it.

Robert J. McCarter, February 2023

ONE
WEDNESDAY

PATTY WALSH slopped more coffee in my cup as she walked by the long, scarred linoleum counter, filling it to exactly halfway, just the way I liked it. Nothing better in this world than hot coffee and nothing worse than lukewarm.

She flashed me a smile, the one that said she knew me and knew me well. Knew me like my mother never had and my ex-wife never wanted to, and that she knew everything I wanted, and even though her maintaining my coffee just the way I liked was all I would get from her today, that I would love it nonetheless.

And I did.

Patty was beautiful, but not in the Hollywood way. She was rushing up on fifty, the vibrance of her wavy red hair was getting worn down by time and the invading grey, her once fit form was burdened with fifteen extra pounds, and her green eyes weren't quite the wattage they used to be. But every time I sat down at the counter of the Carterville Diner, she would greet me with a sunny, "Howdy, Chief," and knew exactly what I wanted to eat and I never ever had to ask for anything.

Whatever I was in the mood for ended up on a plate in front of me just like magic.

And this is as I would expect it. Patty had a power, and her power was knowing what you wanted before even you knew. Rumor has it—and I will admit I've thought about these rumors way more than is proper—that Patty knew everything a man or a woman wanted. Everything. This made Patty so very attractive in ways that Hollywood could never really convey with their illusions. Even without her power, Patty was a real woman working a real job in small-town Arizona, and there is something sexy about that.

"Somethin' on your mind, Henry?" Patty asked after taking care of the rest of the counter and ending up standing in front of me.

I could hear the bacon and sausage my buddy Frank was frying back on the grill and the clink of silverware against the worn white porcelain of the plates. The smell of the place was sheer heaven, all fat laden and caffeinated, so much so that if I stayed here too much longer, I was liable to have a heart attack.

"Just wondering why I can't ever get the courage up to ask you out," I said.

Patty just stared at me, all straight faced, her apron and her black blouse not able to hide the generous portion of curves God had granted her.

She was like that. It did you no good to not say what you were thinking. She knew what you wanted, and if she stopped to ask you, like she had just done with me, it made not a bit of sense to hold back.

A smile slowly lit up her face, pushing up her freckled cheeks and making her eyes bright. She slowly shook her head. "Why, I don't have a clue about that one. You let me know when you figure it out, okay?"

Her smile brightened and then she was gone and all I had was the press of my breakfast in my belly and the buzz of the caffeine to keep me company.

I grabbed my cowboy hat from the stool next to me, stood up, and caught the cook's eye through the pass-through window. Frank Paulson, one of my oldest and best friends. He had a round face, a shaved head, and kind blue eyes. I smiled, he smiled back, and that was enough of a "thank you" between two old friends that had lived their entire lives in a small mountain town in Arizona.

It was a Wednesday morning, so not too many folks in the diner, the high-backed dark green booths and tables mostly empty. A few locals squatting on the round cushioned stools along the long counter where Patty worked, where they knew they could get exactly what they wanted.

The walls had been made over for the tourists with rusted old signs, vintage posters, and other memorabilia from Carterville's past as an Arizona mining town and Grand Canyon gateway. Things like "Last Gas Before the Grand Canyon" or "Carterville: Visit a Real Working Silver Mine!" or an enlarged newspaper headline from 1926: "Is the Carterville Sawmill Really Haunted?"

I knew all the locals, but it was still easy to spot the tourists. They had on shorts and flip-flops and kept whispering and gawking, eyeing the locals and talking to each other in hushed tones which I didn't need to hear to know what they were asking.

I put on my aviator sunglasses—the cheap ones, I'll have you know, not Ray-Bans—and tried to escape with my happy belly and the hope that Patty's smile had given me still intact.

"Officer, excuse me."

I suppressed a sigh and turned to the booth I had just walked past. It appeared to be two couples, all of them millennials with their pricey phones, smart watches, and colorful T-shirts that didn't come in packs of three from Wal-Mart. The woman that spoke to me had long blond hair and a smile bright enough to make me want to keep my sunglasses on. She was drenched in a perfume so strong, I couldn't smell bacon or coffee and that just made me sad. Her wrist was festooned with brass rings that jingled when she gestured.

"Yes, ma'am?" I said, keeping my tone short and clipped.

"Well… we…" her blue eyes darted away, looking at Patty and old Mary Reilly alone in a booth on the other side of the diner and then back to me.

The blonde was sitting next to a sandy-haired boy all muscular and sure of himself, his plain black T-shirt silky smooth and tight, his overworked biceps on display. "What Raven is trying to ask," he began, and then his eyes wouldn't meet mine either.

I knew what they wanted to ask. It was what everyone wanted to ask.

"Is it true?" Raven piped back in, the name making me wonder how many chemicals were involved in her surfer-girl-blonde hair.

"Ma'am?" I asked. I wasn't going to make this easy on them.

Bicep-boy jumped in and asked, "Is it true you all have…

you know… superpowers? That everyone that lived here that day got them… is it true?"

I couldn't suppress the sigh this time. These kids had cut their teeth on the never-ending glut of Marvel movies and TV shows. They wanted to believe it was all romantic like that, everything happening on well-lit sets with heroic deeds done by Hollywood beautiful people with everything made CGI perfect.

"Mostly," I said, "although I don't know I would call them 'super.' A few of us didn't get powers, and between you and me, that's just fine."

"You didn't…?" Raven mumbled, the look of horror on her face almost making my day. She couldn't imagine how I could be okay with being skipped over.

"Now if you all will excuse me…" I nodded my head, put my cowboy hat on, and walked out the diner, the bell on the door ringing as I went out into the cool, sunny morning still trying to hold Patty's smile close to my heart.

I had been lying to them, of course. I did have a power, but I wouldn't call it "super," and it wasn't the kind of thing you shared with strangers, or the kind of thing you even shared with friends, not if you were smart. I'm sure Patty knew about it, but I didn't think anyone else did. Or at least I hoped.

———

FROM THE OUTSIDE, THE CARTERVILLE DINER WAS JUST ABOUT as plain as the rest of our little town. It was a squat, old brick building on Main Street, sandwiched between two other old brick buildings. Except for the fifties-style neon sign marking it as "The Carterville Dinner," it was just another quaint brick building.

To the south, rising above the town, were the sharp slopes of the San Francisco Peaks featuring the twelve-thousand-foot Mount Humphreys which rises well above the tree line. The diner is about halfway up Carter Hill, but from the top you can see the inner basin, a huge scoop out of the volcanic mountain, filled with aspen, spruce, and fir.

It is theorized that Humphreys and Agassiz, the main two peaks you always see in the logos around this mountain, used to form one single seventeen-thousand-foot peak before the volcano that it used to be blew its top off creating the inner basin and making the mountain a whole lot shorter.

I sometimes worry that this town will do the same. Carterville has only 286 permanent residents, but with 198 of us with some kind of power, as strange as many of them are, it seems like a recipe for disaster.

This is the kind of thing I tell myself, and then I tell myself that I won't run for chief of police again, and then I do.

I guess I lie to myself sometimes.

And I guess that makes me human.

I took a deep breath of the cool air trying to shake the thought off, the pungent scent of the junipers reminding me of gin, but the day was just getting started.

I'd like to say that I have avoided the pernicious trap of cliché, that I am a middle-aged white man that didn't have a slowly expanding bulge around my waist, that didn't drink just a little too much to palliate the difficulties of my day, that didn't have a receding hairline and the implacable invasion of grey in my mousey brown hair.

But that wouldn't be true, and as an officer of the law,

dutifully elected by the voters of Carterville, Arizona, I feel that I must tell the truth. I do have that belly and enjoy my gin, and what hair I have left seems to be getting greyer every day.

And my job as the police chief of a small town seems to be getting harder every day. What with the "Incident" that transformed the residents of Carterville, things just keep getting crazier and crazier.

But my name is Henry Carter and this town is named after my ancestor, Samuel Carter, who first discovered silver here in the late 1800s. That heritage is something I'm proud of. Carters have been living and working and dying here for one hundred and thirty-eight years.

It's not like I can leave.

It's not like I know anything else.

Even though I don't really know my little town anymore.

Those tourists in the diner, Raven and Bicep-boy and their friends, they are here hoping that somehow the Carter Powers rub off on them, except they ain't gotta clue how it happened.

All they know is that Carterville residents have powers (super or not), but only if they are within five miles of the town. Outside that radius, we all are as normal as the next person. When I go to Phoenix to visit my son, I'm just a middle-aged man with knees that get creakier every day. Well, hell, my powers have nothing to do with my knees, so that happens here, but you get what I mean.

Tourists come hoping they can have powers for a day, even though it doesn't work that way. And the mayor doesn't do a thing to dissuade that perception. Frankly, Carterville hasn't been this busy since silver was being pulled out of the ground and people arrived by stagecoach and on horseback.

Some of the rumors of Carterville powers mention the meteorite, the one that crashed through the remains of one of the mineshafts, and they aren't completely wrong.

On that cold October night, the stars bright above us, the ground shook and the sound of the impact woke us all up. We all thought it was a quake.

None of us knew, of course, that anything had happened. Patty, who always thought of herself as intuitive, just started knowing what everyone wanted the next day. A lot of folks didn't realize what their powers were until something happened, until something triggered it. Or, like me, until enough bizarre things happened that they finally put it together.

And now I know you are wondering what my mysterious powers are. Just be patient. My grandpa taught me that stories have to find their own way, in their own time, so we'll get there. I promise you, it's finally time to talk about them and I will.

Carterville is built on a hill, Main Street quite steep for most of its length, but this affords you with one of the best parts of Carterville—the view.

I turned to the north, and squinting, I could see the distant cut in the desert that marked the Grand Canyon. To the east rose the cinder cone of Sunset Crater and beyond that the cinder crater field that makes it abundantly clear just how this mountain rose out of the desert.

Depending on where you are on the hill, Carterville is between 6,400 and 7,100 feet in elevation with the towering mountain behind us, the vast desert in front of us, and the ponderosa pine, juniper, and piñon pine trees all around us. The sun shines three hundred days a year, the air is clean, and the skies are blue.

Main street is just getting steep here at the diner with sidewalks on either side and mature fir and maple trees lining the street.

I was born in Carterville, and it's been my home nearly all of my life. It's all very familiar but I still see the beauty, I still love it, and I'm still so glad to be here. I was taking it all in, getting ready to step onto Main Street and cross over to the police station when a scream emanated from the diner.

A woman's voice.

Patty.

I didn't think. I ran back in.

———

EXCEPT FOR THE PEOPLE I PASSED RUNNING OUT, IT LOOKED almost normal for a Wednesday morning. People sitting in a few high-backed booths, the smell of bacon and coffee making me wish I wasn't already at my limit. But then I heard Patty crying from the back and saw Raven, the blond, flip-flopped tourist girl standing behind the counter, her hand on her mouth as she stared into the kitchen. Mary Reilly, still in her booth, gave me a wide-eyed look like a deer caught in headlights. She was nearly eighty years old, grey haired and tiny, the booth nearly swallowing her.

I pulled the radio from my belt. "Dispatch, this is Carter. We've got a situation at the diner. Send backup."

"Roger that, Henry," Annabelle replied. "Y'all okay?" There was a tone to Annabelle's voice. Her lovely southern drawl was there, but she'd been working dispatch for the past seven years, since before the meteor hit, since the Incident, and there was something weary there too, like she knew that none of us were really okay anymore.

I pulled my taser and eased back behind the counter, past the wide-eyed Raven and into the kitchen. Bacon was sizzling on the wide grill and pancakes were burning. Big Frank Paulson was laid out on the greasy linoleum floor, a bloody hole in his back. Patty was squatting next to him crying. She was clearly in shock. Her empathetic power didn't always help in an emergency. And Bicep-boy was standing, his back to the griddle with a bloody knife in his hand and a blank look on his face.

Shit!

"Drop the knife, son," I said, calmly, evenly. "You have to the count of three." The boy had a smear of blood on his lips and his chin, and I wished for the millionth time the world didn't know about us. There was a rumor that the blood of a Carterville powered person could convey their powers to you.

Christ, the world can be so stupid sometimes. It seemed like most of the time, anymore.

I didn't have time for any of this. Frank was bleeding out. Frank needed help. But I needed to stop anyone else from getting stabbed.

"One..." I said. Bicep-boy's brown eyes were vacant, maybe he was in shock. "Two..." He didn't acknowledge me and just stared at Frank unblinkingly, licking his bloody lips, the knife held like he was ready to stab again. "Three..." No movement. No nothing.

I fired the taser. He convulsed and went down hard, the

knife clattering to the floor with him. Raven was shouting, but I ignored her and grabbed my radio. "Annabelle, we need the doctor here, and now, and call for an ambulance! Reroute Officer Ortega and have her go bring Smitty here. Hurry!"

Annabelle was saying something, but I was too busy to really hear her, my heart thumping in my chest. I rolled Bicep-boy over and cuffed him, and then I went to Frank.

He's a big man, a good two hundred and fifty pounds. He was born here, just like me. We went to high school together in Flagstaff (Carterville's not big enough for its own). He was still married to his first love. He had three kids, two grand-kids. And he had a power, just like the rest of us.

Frank had a green thumb. Not literally, of course, but he could grow anything in all but the harshest condition. Much of the produce at the diner was grown in the greenhouse at Frank's place.

He had one of the good powers, really he did. Nothing double-edged about it at all. Well, he really liked plants better than people these days, which made him grumpier than he used to be, but he really did get lucky when that meteorite hit.

Time seemed to slow and my breathing was loud in my ears.

I grabbed a towel hanging on the stainless-steel island Frank prepped his food on. The table held bright green broc-coli heads and perfectly white cauliflower heads, probably destined for his dinner special. The towel was dirty, stained with grease, but I bunched it up and pressed it to Frank's wound, my knees in the growing puddle of his blood.

Raven ran to Bicep-boy, tears running down her face.

I heard a commotion as the other couple that had been at the booth with Raven and Bicep-boy tried to get back into the kitchen. Old Mary Reilly told them to go sit back down, a growl and a lot of power in her old voice, and they did. And fast. They had no choice, really, although they probably wouldn't remember it that way.

I was glad Mary was out there with her power at the ready.

Patty was sobbing, hard, but I ignored her—there was nothing I could do for her.

I pressed the towel against his wound, trying desperately to slow the flow of blood. I could feel it pulsing underneath my now blood-soaked hands, the smell of it driving out the bacon and coffee smell of the kitchen, and I was regretting my big breakfast.

If the knife had hit his heart or pierced an artery, there would be nothing a doctor could do, and judging by how quickly it was pouring out, there was little doubt. A hospital might be able to help him, but we are forty minutes away from Flagstaff and the ambulance would have to get here first.

Frank's only hope was Smitty.

I caught Patty's wide eyes. She stopped crying and blinked and then nodded. She knew.

She knew that I needed Frank to live and that Smitty was his only hope. She knew it wasn't going to be easy.

I heard the warbling of a siren getting closer. That would be Officer Ortega with Smitty.

Patty sniffed and nodded and pursed her lips, her eyes staying connected to mine. Right then I knew what she wanted, and it was the same thing I wanted, for Frank to live.

She put a smile on her face, but it was shaky and barely

there. It wasn't fair, but if anyone could understand what Winston "Smitty" Smith wanted, it was Patty.

I prayed to a god I didn't believe in anymore and pressed on Frank's wound.

———

Winston "Smitty" Smith was tall, thin, and all angles. His nose was sharp, his hazel eyes dull, and his scraggly blond hair was way too grey for his thirty-six years.

He had beads around his neck, wore loose flowing linen clothing, and looked like he belonged in New Age Sedona, not old-fashioned Carterville.

Smitty has a superpower. A real live superpower. The doctor, Jenny Lion, was back in the kitchen with Frank, but I didn't need powers to read the dire look on her face and to know she wasn't going to be able to save him. Officer Ortega was helping the doctor and keeping an eye on Raven and the still-unconscious Bicep-boy.

Mary Reilly was still there, all four-foot-four of her, a grim look on her wrinkled face, her pink lips pressed into a thin line. I nodded to her—she had cleared the rest of the diner out and I was grateful. She wasn't exactly an official member of the department, but she was smart and would step in with crowd control and the like when I needed her. No one would think that a grey-haired grandma that always wore a pleated skirt and a sweater she had knitted herself could demand such obedience.

You didn't get on Mary's bad side, what with her power.

I was walking slowly, rubbing Frank's blood off my hands, wishing I could smell anything else. My heart was pounding in my chest and I had no patience for what needed to be done. Patty was standing next to Smitty, her green eyes looking haunted.

"Smitty," I said with a nod.

"Chief," he growled.

Before all this power stuff, Smitty was a part-time mechanic and full-time petty thief. He didn't wear guru clothing then, but jeans and flannel shirts. I had arrested him many times, but never had enough to put him away for very long. There was no love lost between us. Especially not since the meteor hit and he had gotten a power that was super.

A lot had happened between us in the last few years. To say that we had "history" was a ridiculous understatement. To say there was "bad blood" was not even covering the half of it.

"Patty told you," I said, not a question.

He nodded.

"Will you do it?" I asked.

He shrugged his shoulders and I just wanted to punch him.

I glanced at Patty and she frowned and her brow furrowed. Whatever he wanted, it was too much.

"What do you want?" I asked. There was no time for niceties.

"You know what it costs me," he said dryly, dodging the question. And I did, from personal experience. Smitty's superpower was healing. If the person wasn't dead, he could bring them back. But at a cost, which his premature grey attested to.

"What do you want?" I repeated.

He sighed and Patty wouldn't meet my eyes.

I took a step forward until I was close enough to smell the

patchouli oil he always wore these days. "Goddammit, Smitty! Spit it out. Frank doesn't have any time."

He blinked, slowly, and then a smug grin spread on his face. "I want you to leave Carterville and never come back," he said. "You do that, you promise me, then I'll save Frank."

I stepped back, almost stumbled, my heart beating loud in my head, my nose full of Smitty's patchouli mixing with the scent of blood and the distant odor of what was burning on the grill.

He wanted me to leave my home. The home of my family since the mine was started. Where my son was born. Everything I knew. Everything I loved.

"I'll need a month to wrap things up," I heard myself saying. My voice was calm, way too calm, and I didn't recall actually making a decision.

"You got a week," he sneered.

"Done! You save Frank, I'll be out of here in a week. I promise." I grabbed him by the arm and shoved him back towards the kitchen, my heart still a loud whooshing in my head.

Patty just stared at me, a mixture of relief and pity on her face. She knew I would do it, she knew exactly how hard this would be for me, so much so that she hadn't considered it an option. Even with her power she hadn't thought I would do it.

Everything has its limits.

But Frank. I had to help Frank.

———

I've got a telescope on my deck. Sure, I use it to look at the stars or the moon, but I use it during the day to peek at the Grand Canyon or Sunset Crater, or the Painted Desert or any of a dozen other beautiful places in this Northern Arizona desert.

My house is odd. The original cabin is over a hundred years old, but my ancestors added on to it every few decades. An indoor bathroom, a real kitchen, a bigger bedroom, a large deck. Leaving it this strange amalgam with lots of odd turns and corners and little steps up or down.

The old wood siding is encased in worn white vinyl, a gift of the fifties, and the hardwood floors creak when you walk on them. But it's the deck and the view that is the star when the weather is the least bit tolerable.

I left Ortega to deal with Malcom Bishop, aka Bicep-boy. Smitty did his part and Frank was alive. He was airlifted to the Flagstaff Medical Center. He lost an awful lot of blood and even Smitty's power has its limits, but it looked like he was going to make it.

I should have been back at the station dealing with all of this, but I just couldn't. I promised Smitty I would leave if he saved Frank. He did. I couldn't stand the thought of leaving.

The sun was easing towards the west and a chilly September breeze had kicked up. I was slouched in an Adirondack chair so old, the wood was bleached to a flat silver, my hand clutching my drink a bit too hard. It was my favorite, gin and soda on ice with a squeeze of lime and a dash of bitters, but I kept eyeing it suspiciously, trying to focus on the view.

In many ways this view was Carterville to me. My father had built the deck when I was eight. I helped him. I've re-stained and resealed it many times. I rebuilt it three years ago.

I shared the house with my sister. She worked at the

Flagstaff Medical Center, three twelves a week and stayed with her daughter and grandchild there when she was working and was here the other nights. She was there today and I texted her about Frank and she said she would keep me updated.

I didn't tell her about the deal I made with Smitty.

I hadn't told anyone, but this being a small rural town, most everyone knew by now.

My brain wasn't working right. Leaving was just too big a thought to hold on to. Sure, when I was a teenager, I wanted to get the hell out. I went to college in San Diego, and as nice as the ocean and the warm weather was, I couldn't stand all the people. I loved looking at the ocean, but for me it lacked the character and diversity of sitting here and staring at this desert.

I got my first job as a police officer in Tucson, and while I was so happy to be back in Arizona, the city was just too big for me, too many people, too many murders.

I'm a small-town boy. A Carterville boy. I came back and worked under the old police chief until he retired, and then I ran for and got his job.

I set the drink down on the arm of the Adirondack, my hand was getting cold. I hadn't imbibed yet, because I figured once I did, it would be a long time until I stopped, and I still needed to think.

"Excuse me, Boss."

I nearly jumped out of my skin and turned to see Officer Isabella Ortega. Short, young, and stocky with warm brown eyes and a ready smile. She was in her navy-blue uniform with her long black hair pulled back into a ponytail. She stood nervously shifting her weight from foot to foot. She was a third-generation Mexican immigrant, but her grandmother was Navajo and she spoke the language, along with Spanish, making her extra useful since we were close to the reservation.

"Shit, Ortega," I said as I pushed myself up. I was still in my uniform but had changed out of my bloody pants and locked my gun belt away in the safe. "You about scared me to death. Can't you see I'm gettin' ready to get good and drunk?"

She looked down. The girl was smart, capable, driven, but unaccountably shy. She wasn't a Carterville native, wasn't here for the Incident, and had only been here a few years. Why she wanted to live and work in this crazy town, I hadn't figured out yet. A few years ago, she helped out on a tough case as a Coconino County sheriff's deputy and had wanted to stay.

"Sorry…" I said with a sigh. "Bad day. What's up?"

"I tried radioing…" she said by way of apology.

"You're good, Ortega. Spit it out."

"The perp, Bishop, says he has no recollection of what happened. Claims he never heard 'The Blood of Carterville' legend."

I shrugged. "He was there. Patty saw it. I saw him holding the knife. He had Frank's blood smeared on his face."

She pursed her lips. "The girlfriend backed him up in independent questioning as did the other couple that was with them."

I sighed and walked to the edge of the deck and leaned on the railing. Below me houses lined the steep hill Carterville was built on, giving me an unobstructed view of the desert.

"And…" I prompted. She had something else. I knew her well enough to know that.

"Mary Reilly told him to tell the truth," she said.

It wasn't protocol, using powers like that on the job, but sometimes we didn't really have a choice. "And…" I tried not to make it a growl, I just didn't have any patience left.

"He said that he blacked out shortly after you left and came to on the floor of the kitchen."

Shit!

I was never fond of mysteries, but in a town with nearly two hundred people with powers, some strange, some super, I just plain hated them. It could have been worse, but some have had enough and left Carterville and their powers behind.

"Well, let's get into it then," I said, leaving my drink and my view behind. I had a week left, might as well solve one more case.

———

I READ SOME COMICS AS A KID, THOUGHT A BIT ABOUT WHAT kind of superpower I would want to have. Flying sounded good, but seemed too dangerous, so many ways for that to go bad. Being really strong would be nice, but again, that kind of power can go sideways in an instant. I settled on invisibility. Yeah, I was a shy kid. Being able to truly hide or spy without being caught had a certain kind of appeal. Anonymity as a superpower, now that can make you feel safe.

Oddly, the day the meteor hit, someone did gain that power, sort of. Martin Lester was a former officer of mine but a murder a couple of years ago and his actions in the aftermath forced me to fire him and he left Carterville. Martin wasn't "invisible," per se, his power made it so he was very hard to see if he didn't want to be seen. He wasn't invisible, he'd show up in photographs, but people just wouldn't notice him.

That day, I really wished that I had Martin's power, that I could use it and stay in my home and no one would know.

Ortega drove us down to Cedar Street—the station was just east of Main. It took all of a minute. Carterville really is a small town. We've only got the one police vehicle, a used Ford SUV we bought from the Phoenix PD a few years ago. She uses it more than I do and it was a mess, full of junk food wrappers and empty coffee cups and it smelled like congealed French fries. I didn't have the energy to chew her out about it. The girl was a slob, and nothing I had ever said had changed that.

We didn't talk on the way, which suited me.

Our offices are in the back of what was the original Carterville post office. A two-story brick building that is as plain as the day is long. The front of the building, which faces Main, is a bakery, the back half, which you access from Cedar, is our place, the top floor is some offices.

It smelled like bread and sweets all day long, which hadn't been good for my waistline.

We've got one big room with three desks, filing cabinets, and a large whiteboard that has notes about recent calls. There was a jumble of evidence bags on Ortega's desk. The knife, still bloody, and some sample vials, clearly from the perp. Probably some from Frank, and that thought just made my stomach turn. Ortega was nothing if not thorough.

The back room has two holding cells and there's a separate room, not much more than a big closet, that serves as my office and the armory. The walls were white. The fluorescents were too bright. And the floor was scarred linoleum.

Annabelle Unger was sitting at her desk along the wall near the whiteboard. She's a few years older than me, getting close to sixty, but was tall and slim and her hair was bright red with streaks of purple (chemically aided, of course). She's our dispatcher and office manager. She doesn't wear a uniform, although I would really like her to, and was in her usual tight jeans and sweater with high heels.

I nodded to her but she wouldn't meet my eyes. She knew what I had promised to do. She knew I kept my promises. "You two get into the database," I said. "Find me some suspects with the right powers." It came out more clipped than I would have liked. "Please" and "thank you" go a long way to making life a lot more pleasant, but it had been a day.

And the database I was referring to was really a spreadsheet that Annabelle had compiled that had all the residents and their known or suspected powers.

I didn't wait for them to reply. I headed back to the holding cells.

In the left one, Malcom Bishop sat and in the right was Raven Reynolds. His cell was locked, hers was not. They were holding hands through the bars. The couple that had been with them had given their statements and had hopefully found a room to stay in, Ortega having told them to not leave town.

Bishop still had blood staining his hands and a haunted look on his face. Somehow his biceps bulging in his plain black T-shirt didn't look so big anymore.

"Come on," I said, pulling my keys from my belt and unlocking his cell. "I bet you would like to clean yourself up."

He slowly looked up at me and nodded. I saw a flatness to

his brown eyes that looked like shock to me. He stood and so did his girlfriend, their hands still clasped through the bars.

"Ms. Reynolds," I said. "Please wait here. We'll be right back."

She nodded absently and sat back down on the cot.

I guided the young man out into the main room and into the men's bathroom. I stood against the door while he used one of the stalls and then stumbled to the sink and started washing his hands.

He did it once, twice, and on the third time I just shook my head. His hands were shaking, his eyes weren't right. I was starting to believe his story.

"You okay, son?" I asked.

He turned and looked at me, startled, like he had forgotten I was there. He nodded weakly.

"Can you tell me what happened?"

He nodded again, but didn't say anything, washing his hands for another few minutes. When he finally stopped, he turned and glanced at me and then stared at his hands. They were red from being washed so much and water was dripping off them onto the old brown linoleum.

"Jeff, he was going on about powers, about this place…" he began, and then he bit his lip. "It was his idea, you know. Go look at the Carterville freaks."

I cringed inside, but I tried not to let it show. I nodded for him to continue.

"We had just talked to you and Jeff was freaked that you didn't have powers, that you were just fine with it. He was going on and on and then his voice got distant, like he was at the other end of a tunnel. And… and… I felt numb. I mean, not numb, but like my body wasn't mine anymore. You know what I mean?"

I didn't, but I did my best to smile and nodded.

"I remember standing up. I think I said something about the bathroom. And I don't remember anything until I woke up handcuffed with… with…" He was staring at his hands again.

I felt sorry for the kid and I more than half believed him. But he was still a suspect, we still had witnesses and evidence. In any other town it would be enough, we would be done, but not in Carterville.

I took his arm and guided him back to his cell and locked him in.

"What… what's going to happen to me?" he asked, his voice sounding like a scared little boy's.

"We're going to find who did this," I said. I didn't really answer his question because I didn't have a good answer for him. I didn't have any answers, only questions.

TWO
FRIDAY

My head hurt. Bad. Throbbing with my heartbeat. My tongue was thick and sticky and it felt like someone had stuck needles into my desert-dry eyes.

I finally had gotten a chance to get good and drunk out on my deck last night watching the sun set over the desert and then watching the stars twinkle to life until the Milky Way was strewn above me, glittering and alive.

"You okay, Boss?" Ortega asked, putting a mug of steaming black coffee in front of me and sitting in the chair across from my beaten and battered metal desk in my tiny windowless office.

I groaned.

She put down a glass of water and three aspirin.

I shot the aspirin back with the entire glass of water, sipped the coffee, burned my tongue, and groaned again.

Despite knowing everyone in town, I got drunk alone. I

don't find my own self-pity to be pretty at all, and it is not something I want to share.

"Smitty was by before you came in," Ortega said, her voice calm like she was telling me about the weather. "He said you got five days left."

I ground my teeth together and took a deep breath, fighting down my nausea. Ortega was playing me, I wasn't hungover enough to not see that, but I appreciated it.

"So who do we have left?" I asked, getting a little more coffee down. Much of Wednesday and all of Thursday had been spent dealing with the crime scene, checking powers, seeing who was in town, and trying to find someone who could have taken Malcom Bishop over and stabbed Frank.

And trying to come up with a motive. Frank was well loved and the whole town was missing the diner. It was kind of the hub of our little town. The town council held meetings there. Everyone ate there.

"We got three folks to talk to today," Ortega said. "Everyone else has been ruled out." Her mouth was twisted into a half frown.

"And…" I prompted.

She shook her head. "Their powers are kind of close but… not quite right to pull off what happened to Bishop."

I nodded and sipped some more coffee, starting to feel the beginnings of its effect and knowing that this was a day where there simply wouldn't be enough coffee.

———

"Tell Smitty to go to hell," Frank said on my phone. Ortega was gone and I had the door closed. The coffee had made me feel vaguely human, if a bit strung out. Frank sounded weak as a kitten, but hearing his voice lightened my heart. "I'm the one who owes him, don't leave, Henry. God, please don't leave."

He would blame himself if I did.

"A deal's a deal," I said, my voice coming out weaker than I wanted it to.

"Bullshit!" Frank spat weakly back. "Not with him. No, not with *him*."

There was history. A small town like this and everyone has some sort of history. About fifteen years ago there was a break-in at the diner. Frank had taken the young Smitty under his wing, was teaching him to cook, was hoping the kid could take over for him one day.

Frank is a collector of Civil War memorabilia. Some of it pretty pricey. The day of the break-in, a package had come in the mail and the postman, knowing Frank and guessing what it was, brought it to the diner, but he was out and Smitty was manning the grill.

That night, someone threw a rock through the front door, levered open the register, which only had a few bucks in it, and took the package.

Everyone knew Smitty did it, but we had no evidence.

Frank fired him and two months later Frank's house was robbed of… you guessed it, all of Frank's valuable Civil War memorabilia.

The problem with Smitty has always been his lack of morals and his abundance of intelligence. His superpower had only made that worse.

"Maybe I'll move to Flagstaff," I said gently. "Forty minutes away."

"But why?" he hissed. "Why would you keep your word to

that… that… man?"

"Don't make me answer that question, Frank," I said.

"Why? Tell me!"

I sat there with the phone to my ear, my head throbbing and my mouth dry. Smitty had saved my life a couple times over the last few years, and I, in turn, had returned the favor a couple of times, so there was nothing I owed him and nothing he owed me. All that was left between us was bad blood and plentiful dislike.

So, why would I keep my word beyond trying to be an honorable human being, beyond the fact that Smitty had saved Frank's life, beyond me sometimes wondering what a life away from Carterville and all this madness would be like?

"You are Henry Carter," he said quietly. "There is no Carterville without you."

He was overstating it, but I appreciated the sentiment.

"Not on the phone, Frank," I said. "I can't talk about this on the phone. Not today. When you are back, okay? I'll tell you then."

He took a deep breath and sighed. "Yeah. Another day or two and I'll be back. You will tell me, Henry. You *will* tell me."

———

THE MAIN STREET OF CARTERVILLE RUNS UP CARTER HILL, AND it's a steep hill going from mild at the bottom, quickly to extreme at the top. The entire town is draped on the north-facing side of Carter Hill, a lump of earth that was ejected from the San Francisco Peaks long ago when it blew its top like Mount Saint Helens did in 1980.

If you walk south on Main Street, it's going to be some

exercise, and I was in no mood for exercise, but it didn't make sense to drive a block and a half, even if it was uphill.

Not that where we were going was far from the police station, it wasn't. Ortega and I had walked down to the diner to check on things. It was locked tight, and everything was fine. Seeing it that way was a gut punch but not as much of one as was coming. Since we had walked down, we had to walk back up.

The difficulty of the walk was somewhat compensated by the view. Walking uphill you can see the mountain peaks, and if you are walking downhill you are rewarded with the pastel colors of the desert.

But today, I hardly noticed the view. With each step, my heart sped up and my blood pressure rose and the pain behind my eyes got worse with each beat of my heart.

I didn't exactly regret getting drunk. I had good cause and it had been a lovely night to be outside, but I wasn't exactly thrilled by the fallout. I should have stayed home, maybe started packing, but my sister was coming back, and judging from our brief phone call, she was a lot more angry and way more confused about this than Frank was.

At least I could show her that I had gotten some floors in on my fitness tracker. The one she gave me after my heart scare a few years ago. The one I hated with every fiber of my being. And then I remembered, I was wearing that damn cheap piece of plastic on my wrist, but the battery had run down at least a week ago.

"You up for this, Boss?" Ortega asked.

She was, very diplomatically, asking about a bit of my history we were about to run into. A five-foot-four fireball of a bit of my history.

I grunted and nodded and kept going. People were staring at me, locals that is. They all knew that I was going to honor my promise to Smitty and leave the town that bore my name. Leave it without its chief of police.

They thought I was crazy.

They thought I was stupid.

I'm sure Ortega did too, but she was too smart or too shy to say anything.

Annie Smith wouldn't be either.

———

"Well look what the cat drug in," Annie Smith drawled from behind the reception desk of the Carterville Inn. "The heart, and goddamn soul, of Carterville itself."

The three-story red brick building was originally built in 1890. It had nice touches such as arched windows and stamped tin on the ceiling of the first floor. The lobby was filled with large black-and-white prints of turn-of-the century Carterville. The "reception desk" was the original wooden bar that was installed here, its first use being as a saloon.

The inn was on Carterville Circle, the roundabout situated on a flat section of Carter Hill that connected Main Street with Cedar and was the center of our town.

Annie Smith was a petite five-foot-four with hair as black as midnight, high cheekbones, and piercing blue eyes. Her skin was well tanned, and although she had the wrinkles of her fifty or so years, they weren't very noticeable except for deep frown lines. She had a white dress shirt with a thin black tie and a black vest on.

She was also the first woman I fell for in high school and the first woman I dated after my divorce. We tried twice, decades apart, and both times it didn't end well.

Actually, it's more complicated than that. We tried once in high school, but after my divorce we had been on again, off again for years until a couple of years ago when Annie became a suspect in a murder investigation.

We had been doing good, but she had been a real suspect and you can just imagine how that might taint an already tenuous relationship.

I plastered a smile on my face and said, "Good to see you too, Annie."

She snorted. "And I hear I won't be seeing you around here for much longer."

"And I know that makes you very happy," I said with the sweetest smile my hangover would allow.

"That it does, cowboy," she said with a smile so sharp it could cut glass.

"Ms. Smith," Ortega said, taking a step closer to the bar. "We've got a few questions for you."

She didn't look at Ortega, her eyes drilling into me instead, and with the hangover it felt like that was what she was literally doing. She nodded slowly. "I heard you all were considering powers with what happened to Frank." She sighed and her face softened. "I'm glad that old bastard is going to make it."

Frank and Annie dated in high school before she and I did. She's the one thing, throughout all these years, that ever got in the way of our friendship.

"Yeah," I said with a nod. "He's gonna make it. He was just yelling at me a few minutes ago."

Annie smiled for real and it was a hell of a thing to behold. Made me remember why I had wanted to try with her so many times.

"Seems like the only time you come to see me anymore, Henry," she said, "is when you want to accuse me of a crime." She held my eyes, her face taking on a bitter configuration before turning to Ortega. "Questions?"

The hotel has a musty odor to it that fits with its age. It usually doesn't bother me, but for some reason I couldn't smell another thing and just wanted to get out of there. And then I noticed the coffee that was set up down the bar a bit. Not one of those damn single-serve machines, but a nice stainless-steel carafe.

"We have reason to believe powers were involved in what happened to Mr. Paulson," Ortega said.

Annie shot me a look as I walked over to the coffee, but I ignored her and poured myself a cup.

"I thought it was a crazy tourist," she said. "'Blood of Carterville' and all of that."

"We have to consider powers with almost every crime these days," Ortega said diplomatically.

The coffee smelled heavenly. The inn wasn't cheap, so Annie always had good coffee. It drove away the musty scent and helped me focus. Since my heart thing, a coronary artery spasm to be specific, caffeine wasn't the reliable friend it used to be and I had to control my intake, but days like this weren't made for things like that.

"Do you know anyone that can control another person?" I asked Annie.

Her eyes narrowed and she was focused on me. "You mean like Mary Reilly, who I hear was there?"

This was the third time in a few years that Annie had been questioned about a crime. I didn't think she was involved but I had a job to do. "Like that," I said, "but the victim blacks out, is not conscious."

Annie blinked, her eyes narrowed further, and then she turned to Ortega. "I'm sorry, Isabella, but can you please excuse us?"

She didn't wait for an answer, but opened a door behind the reception desk, walked into her office, and turned and looked expectantly at me.

I sighed and took another sip of coffee. There was definitely not going to be enough today.

ANNIE SMITH WAS LEANING ON HER DESK, A MESSY AFFAIR WITH stacks of paper and computer gear covering the simple wooden surface. The office was small, smaller than mine, and the lack of windows made me feel claustrophobic. Her arms were crossed and she was looking pointedly at me. The door was still open.

I turned to close it and Ortega's brown eyes caught mine. I saw only pity in them and wished I had drunk just a bit less last night.

After the door was closed, Annie said, "So I'm really a goddamn suspect, Henry? Again?" She didn't wait for me to answer. "You come into my business and accuse me of hurting Frank. Me! You may have the name Carter, but I was born here, my parents were born here, my grandmother was born here.

"Who the hell do you think you are, Henry Carter? What

possible motive would I have to hurt Frank Paulson even if I did have the power, which I sure as hell don't?"

She went on longer, her voice growing in volume and her language getting more and more colorful.

I stood there in front of the closed door shifting my weight from foot to foot like some kid in the principal's office wishing he could run away.

When she finally wound down, her tanned face was flushed a bit red.

On her wall, behind the desk, was a picture taken in Flagstaff after our high school graduation. It's all the Carterville seniors that year. In the middle of the picture is the beautiful Annie Smith and Frank is to her left and I am to her right. Annie and I were together and happy then. We were young and hopeful and innocent.

"Are you done, Annie?" I asked.

Her nostrils flared, she was clearly not done, but she pursed her lips and nodded.

"I know what your power is," I began, my words slow as I tried to fight through the hangover. "I've experienced them. Many times. The best sleep I've ever had in my life. The deepest. The first time you did, it was a bad day... I had spent it dealing with a fatality out on Highway 89. I couldn't get the images out of my head. I had zero chance of sleeping. But you did your thing and I was just gone. I woke up feeling so good."

She nodded, her head only moving a couple of inches.

"A good power for someone who runs an inn," I continued. "People say they sleep so well here. I see it on Yelp all the time."

Her eyes narrowed and she did another micro nod.

"Now, I figure that is just passive, that you aren't actually putting your guests to sleep," I said. "But you live here. You sleep here. That power rubs off. I know it does."

She blinked and nodded again.

"What I have to wonder, Annie, is have your powers expanded at all?"

She didn't nod. She didn't blink. She just stared at me with her arms crossed, her nostrils flaring.

"Did they, Annie?" I asked. "Can you do anything but make people sleep?"

———

While the residential part of Carterville is on the north side of the hill, the mine is on the south. After the tongue-lashing Annie gave me, where she vigorously asserted that her powers hadn't changed one goddamn bit but that I sure as hell had and wasn't the man she once loved, I stormed out and kept walking up that damn hill.

Ortega fell in line beside me and walked with me.

I marched around the Circle and back on to Main Street. Stomped up to Douglass Street where the hill started to get really steep. Up to Engelmann, the street I lived on, and kept going as the hill got so steep the sidewalk turned into a series of very deep steps. Up to Fir, the highest street on the hill where I marched up the metal stairs that took us to the overlook.

I didn't stop. I didn't notice the view. Even though I was huffing and puffing and sweating hard by then, I marched past the old church, made of local volcanic rock, and to the backside of Carter Hill until I could see the mine that my ancestor, Samuel Carter, had built.

Ortega didn't need to ask me about what Annie had said, her volume loud enough that most of Carterville probably heard.

The climb had hurt, the rising blood pressure causing more pain. But this wasn't my first hangover. The pain got so it was unbearable, but then it finally started to ease up as my body heated up and I sweated the poison out.

Ortega had asked me a couple of questions about where we were going at first, but quickly shut up and easily kept up with me as I huffed and puffed and sweated my way to the top. The girl was short but strong, she lifted weights and I'm sure she can bench-press a hell of a lot more than I can.

It's almost all pine trees up here, the junipers and piñons preferring a lower elevation, the sun warming up their brown bark and their vanilla-like scent perfuming the air.

The mine was fenced off. Tall chain link topped with razor wire. It's best that way. Too many ways to hurt yourself down there. Some company in California owns it now. The Carters weren't in mining for all that long, only about thirty years. Samuel was smart enough to hold on to the saloon and the mercantile and a couple of boarding houses when he sold out.

But I liked the mine. Most of the structures were made of ponderosa pine trees that were harvested off of Carter Hill and the surrounding forest. Tall, gangly structures, many of them slumping with age. Four different shaft towers. Ore conveyances. A few odd buildings here and there for equipment and offices and a smithy. The sawmill that had been built to process all that wood. And the stamp mill that crawled up the hill and was ten stories tall.

At this point it was just an odd jumble of wood and rusting metal. Short pine trees had grown and were threatening to reclaim the land that was clear cut over a century ago.

When I was a kid, I spent a lot of time sneaking through the fence and exploring those buildings. I loved it. I'm sure local kids are still doing it and that just worries me these days.

"What are we doing here, Boss?" Ortega asked gently.

I wished she hadn't said it that way. Like I needed handling. Like I was damaged. But I swallowed that down and looked at her and then turned and pointed to the fourth shaft tower, the one that was on the ground, the wood charred and splintered.

That was where the meteorite hit and dove into the ground underneath us. That's how we all got our powers.

She looked at the remains of the shaft tower and then back at me and shrugged.

Yeah, the meteor was old news. Powers were old news. But someone taking over another human was not old news.

I sighed. "If Bishop is telling the truth," I said, "then maybe something changed. Maybe new powers are emerging. Maybe things are about to get a lot crazier. And…" I couldn't finish the thought.

She studied me, her eyes narrowing, "And you thought by coming up here you might be able to *see* something different?"

Well that just sounded stupid. And it wasn't exactly what I was doing. I really wasn't "thinking," just going on instinct, just wanting to see the tangible evidence of what happened to us and walk off my encounter with Annie. But how was I going to explain that to someone still in their twenties who hadn't been through the tumble cycle of life that long?

"Carter, this is dispatch," my radio squawked. "Carter, come in. Over."

I grabbed the radio. "Go ahead, Annabelle. What's up? Over."

"There's a big wreck on 89 and DPS is a ways off. They're asking if we can respond. Over."

I looked back at the downed shaft tower again. Ortega was right, there was nothing to be gained by standing up here and staring at the past. We had the present to deal with.

THREE
SATURDAY

The rest of Friday was a blur of twisted metal, broken and bleeding bodies, tow trucks, ambulances, and directing traffic. I still can't get the smell of oil and smoke out of my nose. Accidents can be the worst of this kind of job. You just can't unsee that kind of stuff and I didn't have Annie to help me get to sleep after it was all over.

The evening was spent out on the deck quite unsuccessfully trying to explain to my sister why I had promised to leave. And after that, tossing and turning in my bed not doing a very good job of sleeping.

Which is to say that on Saturday morning, we hadn't made any more progress on the case and, with Ortega and Annabelle being off, I was on my own. And considering how little sleep I had gotten, it was best for me to be around humans as little as possible.

Both Annabelle and Ortega had offered to come in on Saturday, the specter of my pending absence looming large.

But I talked them both into getting some rest. When I left, they were going to need it.

I had left the uniform and our police SUV behind and was bouncing down a dirt road in my old Toyota pickup. I was about six miles, as the crow flies, away from Carterville, outside the zone of influence.

It always felt a bit weird to me. Not anything I can really put my finger on, but I could feel when I left it. When my power left me. It was kind of like when the electricity goes out and you become aware of the hum of it that is always going on, but your brain filters it out. Leaving the Carterville power zone is like that—you don't really notice the constant buzz until it is gone.

This area is called "the 40s." A chunk of private land north of Carterville and down the mountain a ways that was divided up into large parcels of around forty acres. All twisty dirt roads, few road signs, no power or other utilities, and lots of privacy.

Everyone out here has a dog or two and a gun or two. The peaks still loom over you, but more distant than in Carterville, and we were down a bit below six thousand feet in elevation, the land covered in short twisty junipers and piñons. Which made me think of gin, which wasn't as pleasant a thought as usual, my hangover gone but not forgotten.

I pulled up to Bo Larson's place and sat in my old pickup truck as his old Lab barked its fool head off and ran around the truck. I checked my cell phone, barely any signal, but it should be enough in case the Coconino Sheriff's Office needed me. When Annabelle is out of the office, emergency calls are routed to them.

"Come on, Yaki," Bo called from the door of his beat-to-hell single-wide trailer. "It's just the chief. You know the chief." He whistled and the dog came running. And Yaki did know me and I'm sure he wouldn't have done me any harm, but it's protocol out here. You respect the dogs and you respect the guns.

Besides the 1970s-era single-wide, Bo had a cement slab covered with a tin roof. Something the original owners had built to park their fifth-wheel under. The roof was rusted and the concrete cracked.

There were a few solar cells set up between the two structures and an outhouse. His truck was there and the water tank he used to haul water in. Most of these places were completely off the grid.

Not a bad way to live, if you asked me. Hard, but all yours. But you can't see the desert from here and I would miss that.

Everywhere you looked were Bo's creations. Huge metal pinwheels turning lazily in the breeze. Spinning metal contraptions that twirled along their vertical axis that could just make you dizzy. Simple whirligigs in the shape of animals and elaborate weather vanes.

Beautiful stuff. All made of scrounged metal. All built to last.

The RV shelter was full of his scrap metal and gear and works in progress.

Bo came out and threw a soup bone that Yaki happily pounced on and started gnawing. He had two beers in his other hand.

I got out and stretched.

"We need a beer for this conversation?" Bo called. He's about twenty-two, short with a barrel chest and mop of curly blonde hair with brown eyes just below his overlong bangs. His face was smudged with dirt and covered in about a week's worth of beard.

I smiled, nodded, and met him at two old lawn chairs that had a good view of the peaks. They sat in front of a well-used fire pit.

"On second thought," he said, eyeing me, "maybe you need coffee more than a beer."

That's the thing about passing the big five-oh, everything shows a hell of a lot more on your face than it used to. If you're tired you suddenly look five or ten years older.

"A beer's good," I said and took the bottle from him. "Nice and cold. I see you have prioritized your use of electricity properly."

He shrugged, it was a casual thing and belied the strength underneath his baggy flannel shirt. You don't wrestle with metal all day and not get strong. "Don't need much for them," he said, gesturing at one of his larger metal constructions with his beer bottle. "Just the fridge and the internet."

I nodded and took a sip and sighed.

I've known Bo since he was a teenager. He's a good kid and I'd love to just sit with him for the day and talk and drink beer and watch his constructions twirl in the breeze, listen to the gentle squeaking of them and the sound of ravens cawing.

"So Frank's gonna make it?" Bo asked, bringing my mission back to me.

I nodded.

"A good thing, that," he said with a nod. "Frank is the best of us."

I nodded again and took a long pull on the beer. It was too damn early to be drinking, but it was just the kind of day when you needed a beer in the morning. And it wasn't gin so it felt good going down.

"So ask your questions, Chief," he said, his voice low.

I looked at him and his eyes were staring up at the mountain. Distant. Back when the meteorite had hit, Bo had been sixteen years old, a recent transplant to Carterville from Los Angeles and absolutely hating it. He got angry, a lot, as teenagers are wont to do. But his power caused his rage to spread to other people.

We had outbreak after outbreak of violence that didn't make any sense. It took us two years to figure out it was him. He was just about out of high school then and the simplest solution would have been for him to just leave the area. But Carterville had gotten to him by then, gotten into his blood.

It's a strange thing. The way locals generally couch it is that if the mountain wants you here, there's little that can take you away. And if the mountain doesn't want you here, there is little you can do to stay.

The mountain wanted Bo Larson.

And I get it. I feel strange when I don't have the San Francisco Peaks in sight. I feel exposed somehow. Vulnerable.

I helped him find this place. He calls the office whenever he comes into town.

"Can I see your thumb?" I asked.

He nodded and showed me his left thumb. It was a bit dirty, but otherwise perfect. Not a scratch. Not a scar. The nail was without blemish. This was in stark contrast to the rest of his hand which was full of scars and scrapes.

"I banged the hell out of it hammering on some metal," he said, making it sound almost like an apology. "Split it wide open. I think I broke the bone. I need my hands."

I nodded. "So you went to see Smitty on Wednesday?"

He nodded. "Called Annabelle when I hit town. Was only there for an hour or so."

"Smitty did a good job," I said.

Bo nodded and snorted.

"How long did it take him?" I asked.

Bo sighed. "All of two minutes… After he made me sit there for a damn hour, my thumb throbbing like hell with each heartbeat."

"And what did he charge you?" I asked.

"Five hundred," he said, sounding deflated. That was a hell of a lot of money for him. "I need my hands," he repeated.

I slouched back in the lawn chair and took another sip and stared up at the mountain. The peaks were bare, the tips a rocky grey. It was early fall and the first snow of the season hadn't come yet.

"Were you there when Officer Ortega came to get him?" I asked.

He was silent for a few breaths, the squeak-squeak of his numerous sculptures seeming loud.

"Yeah… I was there. Do you think I did this?" he asked, his voice quiet. Bo had taken it hard when we figured out his power and what it was doing. What Malcom Bishop did fit with his powers, but not what Bishop experienced. Folks under the influence of Bo's power were always angry. They felt justified in their anger. They knew what they were doing, and when Bo's power was involved, it felt like the right thing to do.

"Were you angry, Bo?" I asked.

He shrugged his wide shoulders. "I was in pain. So much pain."

I licked my lips and nodded. "It doesn't exactly fit, but we have to track everything down. You were there and that kid had no reason to hurt Frank. I hope you understand."

He sighed and leaned forward in his chair until his head was low and he was staring at his feet. "I'm sorry, Henry," he said quietly. "I been doin' my meditations. I haven't been angry for a long time. I…"

I put my hand on his shoulder. Bo was younger than my own son, but I have to admit my feelings toward him were somewhat paternal. And I knew that could be clouding my judgement. "It doesn't all line up," I said. "I'm not at all sure it was your power that did this. I wish I could tell you more. I just need you to promise to not come into Carterville until we get this sorted."

He sniffed and nodded. We sat there for a while longer, but suddenly the beer wasn't nearly a strong enough drink.

Smitty built himself a big new house high up Carter Hill about two years ago. He bought three lots on the topmost street, Fir, plowed over the historic houses, and built himself something made of cement and glass and stainless steel that has just about the best view in town.

It's an eyesore and the glint of the glass caught my eye as I got close to town.

You see, Smitty has done everything he could to monetize his superpower. People fly in from all over the world for his "healing touch." That $500 he charged poor Bo Larson was a drop in the bucket for him. Out of towners pay a lot more. Rumor is that he's starting his own brand of energy drink that has been "blessed" by his healing presence.

I hate the guy. I really do.

I shouldn't have, but I drove into town, straight up Main, and turned on Fir and pulled into his expansive driveway. The walkway was flagstone and the oversized front door was made of slabs of aged pine harvested from the mine.

The door opened when I got there and I glanced up and saw the security cameras. "He is expecting you," a young woman said. She was thin and blonde and beautiful, barefoot and decked out in the same kind of off-white linen garb that he wore. It was like she was an acolyte and I was being ushered into the presence of some guru.

Good thing I don't believe in gurus, especially when one of them is Winston "Smitty" Smith.

She gestured for me to follow and took me to a small room at the back of the house with floor-to-ceiling windows and a view of the desert. I'm guessing you would call this a meditation room. It had blooming orchids—probably Frank's doing—soft music playing, water gurgling over a piece of amber and brown granite, and small cushions on the carpeted floor.

The young woman offered to get me a coconut water, which I refused, and then left, closing the door behind her.

Smitty was sitting cross-legged facing the view, his eyes closed, his breathing slow and even.

I didn't buy the "he is expecting you" a bit. Not by a long-shot. He just had standing orders to say that if I ever showed up. Hell, that was probably a standing order for anyone of note in Carterville to bolster the mystique he was trying so hard to create.

There was a reason Smitty built this house up here. Built it so it didn't fit in. Gleefully dozed over some century-old houses. He was telling everyone this was a new Carterville and that this was "his" Carterville.

His money and influence had kept the mayor, Karen Winslow, in office even after the whole "Destroyer of Carterville" mess. It had come out that Smitty had intentionally addicted people, like the mayor, to his power, and that was only a small part of the "Destroyer" mess. I had expected there to be more fallout, but with Smitty's ability to heal, it's very hard for folks to turn against him.

Karen blamed me for her ugly, messy divorce that was fallout from all of that. If chief of police wasn't an elected position in Carterville, I'm sure she would have fired me long ago.

Smitty had the mayor in his pocket and, undoubtedly, the town council with her. It seemed like I was the only one resisting his influence anymore.

I stood there for five minutes, enjoying the view, trying not to notice it was a bit better than mine, and doing my best to pretend to be patient.

He slowly rose, taking some deep breaths, did some kind of yoga stretch that would have just broken my back, and stood and faced me.

"I hear Frank is doing well," he said mildly, his face in a neutral position.

"Yes he is. That is why I am here. I just wanted to thank you for saving him." It was a lie. I wasn't really sure why I went there, but now that I think on it, I was hoping Smitty would let me off the hook, would say I could stay in Carterville.

What a fool I am.

"That is excellent," he said with a small smile. "I trust, then, that you will keep your word."

"Of course," I said, doing my best to keep my tone as neutral as his. "I am a man of my word."

A smile cracked his face wide, showing over-bleached teeth, and I felt a chill. The smile was predatorial, like a shark opening its mouth to chomp down on its prey. "That's what I like about you, Chief. You *are* a man of your word." He paused, but I had nothing to say to that. "Is there anything else?"

I smiled, hoping it didn't look as fake as his. "No, Smitty. I just wanted to thank you for saving Frank."

When I was walking back to my truck, I could practically feel the security cameras watching me. Something was going on with Smitty. I had an idea… no, just an inkling, not even something I could put into words yet, but something wasn't right. About what happened at the diner. About the deal with Smitty. About Carterville itself.

It was right there, right in front of me, but I was just too damn tired to see it.

———

MARY REILLY LIVES IN A VINTAGE AIRSTREAM DOWN ON THE lower part of Carter Hill. There are two almost-flat lots that she and her husband bought right after the meteor strike and the tourists started finding Carterville again.

She's got six beautifully restored Airstreams there. She lives in one and does vacation rentals out of the other five. With William, her late husband, gone, it's just about too much for her, but she has someone else to do the cleaning these days and seems to be managing.

Unlike Smitty, she kept the trees. A couple of pines, a few junipers, and two huge oak trees someone planted there when the original houses were built. The silver trailers are nestled under the trees with colorful awnings. There's an area to play horseshoes, a swing for the kids, and a high-end grill.

It's neat. It's nice. And it's a little different, just like Carterville.

It was late afternoon when I got there and she invited me to have tea with her.

Her husband died on a Tuesday in July, just last year. A heart attack. I had been working the "Destroyer" case and Mary called me directly. I had gone to get Smitty, and he and I… well, it had already been complicated, but he was at the center of that case, was being threatened, things had gotten even worse between us, and he refused to leave his house. By the time I went down and got William to Smitty, William was gone, past Smitty's abilities.

I felt so bad, but Mary never said a word about it. She grieved her husband and got on with her life. That was just the kind of woman she was.

Smitty and his powers changed how people look at disease, made cheating death seem possible, easy even—if you could pay Smitty's price. I don't think that's been a good thing, really.

We live. We die. It's the natural order of things.

Well, at least it seems like it should be.

And because of Smitty, Mary didn't call 911 first. She called Smitty, and when she couldn't get a hold of Smitty, she called me. Powers like Smitty's just warp things in the strangest ways.

"Is the tea okay, Chief?" Mary asked. "Do you need some honey? I could go get you some honey."

We were sitting under the awning of her Airstream at a picnic table. Her little Pomeranian was staring at us from inside the trailer through the screen door, its pink tongue out while it panted. She had gotten the dog after William died and it seemed like it had helped her.

I looked at the chamomile tea in front of me and shook my head. I don't like chamomile, but honey wouldn't save it for me. What I needed was coffee.

"No, no, Mary," I said, taking a sip of the tea. "I'm just tired. It's been a long few days."

She smiled, making the wrinkles on her cheeks seem to multiply. Her skin was thin and well wrinkled, but her hazel eyes were bright and clear. Mary was pushing eighty, she didn't move as fast as she used to, but not a thing was wrong with her mind... as long as she stayed in the zone of influence. Something about it or about her power counteracted her Alzheimer's. She wouldn't have even known about it but for the long European vacation she and William had taken the summer before his death.

Carterville meant different things to all of us, some more than others, but we all have Carterville in our blood. Mary just doesn't leave anymore.

"So what's on your mind, then?" she asked gently. Mary is very careful not to phrase things as commands, not to put her power behind it.

Just like Smitty, Mary is one of the rarer cases where their power crosses the line into "super." If she had said, "Tell me what's on your mind, Henry," had used my name, had used her power, I would tell her everything that was on my mind. Everything. Even more than I have been writing here.

One of the reasons Mary was an unofficial part of the department was that I had to keep an eye on her. It would be a lot cleaner if she, just like Bo, would leave Carterville. But with her Alzheimer's that would be cruel.

I smiled at her. If Bo was like a son, then she was like a mother. I tried to look out for her, help out with repairs down here when I had time. And, yes, my guilt around William is part of that, but only part. Mary is like a mother to many of us.

"I read your statement about what happened on Wednesday," I began. "It was clear, but I was wondering if we could go over it again."

She nodded, took a sip of her tea. "Mind if I ask why?"

I shrugged. "Something doesn't add up." I leaned close. "I'm worried, Mary. It feels like something is changing for Carterville… and not for the better."

She took my hand and gently squeezed. I marveled at how warm her hands were, how thin the skin was, the blue veins clearly visible. "Okay, then," she said. "I'll tell you everything."

And she did, but it wasn't anything I didn't already know. She was in a booth by herself and saw it all. Saw Malcom Bishop stand up and look confused. Saw him head towards the bathroom and then divert back into the kitchen. Saw Patty, on the other side of the restaurant, notice Bishop and head back to the kitchen after she delivered some meals. Heard Frank and Bishop talking, it sounded friendly, and then she heard Frank scream.

I nodded when she was done. I could see Frank laid out on

the linoleum, blood pouring out of him, hear the bacon frying, smell the burning pancakes and his blood.

I shook it off and looked into Mary's kind eyes. "And you didn't speak to Malcom Bishop, right?"

She blinked and then a compassionate smile lit up her face. "It's okay, Henry. You can ask me whatever you need to. I didn't speak a word to that boy. I love Frank, he's as much a part of this town as you and I are."

I nodded and tried to match her smile, but just couldn't.

———

PATTY WALSH LIVED IN A SMALL STUDIO, A MOTHER-IN-LAW quarters next to a historic brick home. The house was eighty years old, but her studio was only twenty, a narrow building with a green metal roof and tan siding with a couple of crab apple trees out front.

She owned the property, and just like Mary, used the main house as a vacation rental. There's Annie's Carterville Inn and a couple of other more traditional hotels, but the vacation rental thing has taken Carterville over.

It was a cool, dusky evening as I walked around the side, over the nice pavers toward the door, and stopped six feet short.

I was too tired for this. There was too much going on for this. But, really, was there a better reason? With the future so uncertain, shouldn't I just get over myself?

This was Patty, so once I made my decision, once I took a step forward, she opened the door.

Her curly red hair was down, spilling over her shoulders, the grey strands intertwining in a way that was really quite striking. At least to a middle-aged man like me. She was in sweats, had no makeup on, and looked just so beautiful. She had a paint-stained rag in her hands and was wiping them clean. She was a gifted painter and sold some of her paintings of the mountain and the Grand Canyon in one of the local galleries.

Patty just smiled and I stood there like a kid and shoved my hands into my jean pockets. She knew what I wanted to say, but she wasn't going to say it for me.

She crossed her arms and leaned against the doorjamb. I could smell cooking meat and heard the warbling sounds of a jazz trumpet escaping her home.

"You look tired," she finally said.

I nodded. "Yeah. Long few days."

She smiled again.

"Look… I… you know…" I stammered. What was I, fifteen?

She laughed, the sound was musical and light and I actually felt younger, and that felt good.

I took a deep breath. "Can I take you to dinner sometime? In Flagstaff?"

Her eyebrow raised, maybe that part had surprised her. "Because you're moving away or…" she trailed off, her brow furrowing.

"I… I just think I'd like to get to know you away from powers. And yeah… I don't know how much longer I'm going to be here."

Her eyes narrowed and she pursed her lips. "But then I won't know what you want, and you…" she ended in a shrug and a raise of her eyebrow. Either she didn't know what my power was, which I doubted, or she was doing me the kindness of not saying it out loud.

"I... I think that might be better," I said.

She nodded and pushed away from the doorjamb and took a step towards me. God, she was beautiful. With sweats on for a Saturday night at home painting, she was so beautiful.

She crossed the distance between us, put her hand on my chest and said, "I think that's a good idea. Let's do it." She rose up on her tiptoes and kissed me on the cheek and whispered, "I'm glad you finally asked." And then she was gone.

All I was left with was her soapy smell, but that was enough. More than enough.

FOUR

SUNDAY

Hope is a strange thing. After leaving Patty, I was suddenly full of it. Just because she had agreed to go on a date with me—and let's be honest, she had signaled pretty clearly what her answer would be when I finally got up the courage —I was suddenly feeling buoyant. Hopeful. And about twenty years younger.

Hope, being what it is, escaped the borders of my relationship with Patty and invaded my whole outlook on life. Maybe we could figure out what really happened when Malcom Bishop stabbed Frank. Maybe there was a way where I didn't have to leave Carterville forever.

My sister and I had a nice evening. We reminisced about Carterville and our past and stayed away from me leaving. We made grilled cheese and tomato soup, a dish our mother had taught us to love, and watched the stars come out on the deck.

I then slept for eleven hours straight, so on Sunday

morning the clear sky looked bluer, the bird song was more cheerful, and everything was brighter and I was full of hope.

Hope. It's a tricky thing.

I still had an attempted murder and the mystery stemming from it on my hands. I still had promised to leave Carterville forever in three days and hadn't done one bit of packing.

But that's not what I did. I put on my uniform and I walked—yes, walked, what did I say about hope?—down to the station, enjoying the sun, listening to the birds, saying hello to people I saw. I was well rested, not hungover, and getting a lot of odd looks.

I'm not dour or anything. I am friendly. I do know everyone in town, but they aren't used to me being cheerful.

When I got to the station, I was surprised to see Ortega there in her uniform in front of the whiteboard. It usually contains notes that Annabelle makes about open calls. Not high tech, but it's a quiet little town—or at least it used to be. Ortega had drawn boxes and arrows with people's names written inside in blue and their powers written in red.

There was Smitty and his healing superpower; Annie Smith, the mistress of sleep; Bo Larson and his communicable anger; Mary Reilly who could tell people what to do; Frank Paulson and his green thumb; and Malcom Bishop who didn't have any powers.

"But what if he does?" I asked after I had seen the board, pointing at the square with Malcom Bishop written in it. I didn't say hello. I didn't ask her what she was doing here on a Sunday morning or try to talk her into taking another day off. I was grateful not to be alone and we were both in uniform, the dark blue signaled work, so we worked.

"Bishop?" she asked, giving me a puzzled look.

I shrugged and she put a red question mark in his box. "So… maybe he was here when the meteor hit?" she asked.

I nodded. "He would have been a minor, like seventeen. We didn't know what had happened that night. Everyone thought it was an earthquake. Maybe he was here with his parents and they left the next morning. He certainly wouldn't be the first one this happened to."

Her brown eyes narrowed and she just stared at me. Maybe she was looking at the hope. Maybe after real sleep I looked a lot younger than I did yesterday. She had made coffee and there was a box of donuts on the desk, and they hadn't been the first thing I went for, which was out of character.

Ortega riffled through the files and pulled out his statement. She chewed on her lip as she scanned it. She cleared her throat and started reading from it, "Ortega: Have you ever been to Carterville before? Bishop: No… we just thought… you know, it would be fun. Something to do. We were in Sedona for a destination wedding and… you know… too many old folks there. Ortega: Is this your first trip to Arizona? Bishop: Yeah." She put the papers down.

I nodded and went for the coffee. "There's something missing here. Something we aren't seeing."

She riffled through folders again and took some photos and put them up on the board with magnets. The bloody knife. The mugshot of Malcom Bishop with blood smeared over his mouth. Frank Paulson with Smitty crouched over him, his hand on the knife hole in Frank's back and his face tight in concentration.

My stomach turned and I put the coffee down. I can

handle bloody photos, just not bloody photos of my best friend.

That hope that had made the day seem so bright, made me happy to come down this morning thinking there might be an easy solution, fled and fast.

"What if it's exactly what it looks like?" Ortega asked. "What if the perp is lying?"

I nodded. "It is the simplest answer, and they are often correct, but Mary asked him directly and that casts significant doubt. Put it on the board. Let's see what else we can come up with."

And so we did. Coffee, donuts, and crazy theories… and some not so crazy ones. Like Bo Larson's power had changed and the victims of it blacked out. Except he wasn't anywhere near the diner when it happened and his powers had always had a proximity factor… unless that had changed too.

Or, Mary Reilly had done it. But this required her to not be the person we thought she was and for her powers to have expanded too. She didn't speak to the boy, the witness statements seemed to confirm that and jived with what she had told me last night. Ortega even got Malcom Bishop on the phone—he had been transferred to the county lockup in Flagstaff—and he didn't even recall Mary, much less remember talking to her.

"That would mean," Ortega began, her forehead deeply furrowing, "that Mary can control people without speaking to them while causing them to black out. And…"

I pursed my lips and nodded. "And if Mary has lost it, we are all screwed." I thought for a moment and paced the old linoleum floor. "But we don't have any other cases like this.

People blacking out and doing things they wouldn't normally do."

Ortega snorted, "Not unless you count the young Friday night crowd at Humphrey's Bar."

Humphrey's was the "cool" bar in town. Right on Main Street with a dance floor, Karaoke night during the weekdays, and plenty of tourists wanting to party in the town with all the powers.

I smiled. It was a good attempt at a joke, but with my hope having left me, I was feeling the weight of my promise. Even if we solved this case, even if it wasn't Bishop, I was still leaving town come Wednesday morning.

"We've never seen powers change like that," I said, coming back to Mary.

We went back over Annabelle's spreadsheet of powers. We spent another three hours trying to figure out who could have done this. Then we switched to motive. Why would anyone want to hurt Frank Paulson?

We couldn't find the power or the motive, which left Malcom Bishop going to jail, and something about that just didn't sit right with me.

"Are you really going to leave, Boss?" Ortega asked when we were out of coffee and out of steam and I was headed for the door.

"Yeah," I said, turning back to her. "Time to give this a rest and go home."

"No..." she began, her brow furrowed, her brown eyes a bit too wide and her arms folded in front of her. "Leave Carterville, like you promised Smitty."

And then it hit me. If I left... rather, *when* I left, this would all fall on Officer Isabella Ortega. Until a new chief was appointed as interim until the next election. And Karen Winslow would make that appointment and this town would change.

I sighed and sat down on one of the desks. She was still at the whiteboard, marker in hand, the boxes and the arrows joined with our competing theories, all ranked.

I nodded at the board. "Take a picture of that and erase it before Mary comes around and sees it."

She blinked a few times in rapid succession. "Are you really leaving?" She sounded way more like the shy girl I had hired two and a half years ago than the young woman who had been finding herself while serving Carterville. "I need to know."

I smiled, as best I could. I appreciated her not asking me why I was leaving. I am sure she had her theories about my power, but I doubted she thought they were involved.

I nodded slowly and couldn't look her in the eye. "I made a deal. I'm a man of my word. I have to leave."

And then she was hugging me. Fiercely. Smelling of coffee and donuts and soap. I hugged her back. If Bo Larson was like a son, she was certainly like a daughter, and here I was getting ready to abandon her and the town my ancestors had built.

A small town like this is all about family whether you share blood or not.

It was midafternoon when I walked home, the sky not so blue and the bird song not so charming. I just wanted to crack one more case before I had to leave… forever.

Just on the other side of hope is despair. My walk to the station had been downhill and hopeful. My walk home was uphill and despair filled. By the time I got there, I was sweaty, out of breath, and sure that I had made a huge mistake by asking Patty out. We weren't going to solve the case and I was going to leave Carterville and never come back. And that isn't the kind of thing that is good for a relationship.

What was I going to do? Move out to the 40s near Bo Larson with Carterville so close, but not reachable. Stay in the area so I could be close to Patty, but not be with her at the diner or at my house or at the overlook?

And what about Ortega? How could I abandon her to this little town that always seemed to be on the brink anymore? When powers might be changing, when Smitty was rising in his influence, poised to finally make Carterville his town?

When I got home, I shoved it all out of my head. No Patty. No case. No date. No Ortega. My sister had gone back to Flagstaff early, her grandson had a cold and Grandma the nurse was not going to miss that. Besides, I think the elephant in the room was just too much for her to stay.

I ignored the call of gin and started packing. A life lived almost entirely in a single house tends to build up some junk. I had loads of it. I waded in and lost myself to it. I filled my pickup twice. The first load was to the local secondhand store run by the Carterville foodbank, the second was to the dump near Flagstaff.

I worked as hard as I could just to keep the despair at bay. Difficult, sweaty work and I knew I would be sore from it in the morning.

But it wasn't enough on either level. Just a scratching of the surface of my life here. There was no way I could put this in any semblance of order before leaving. And the effort couldn't hold the despair at bay either, it kept nibbling at the edges of my consciousness, a low-level hum that just wouldn't go away.

After the dump, on the way out of Flagstaff, I grabbed a burger and some fries and then pulled off 89 at the Carterville exit and just sat there watching the sunset.

The view was terrible compared to Carterville. The exit is in a bit of a valley with dense junipers and piñons and you can't see the desert at all, but I could at least watch the light at play on the northern side of the peaks. It seemed like a metaphor for my future, so close but cut off from what I loved the most.

The food was cold by the time I ate it and tasted about as good as cardboard. But I dutifully chewed and marinated in my despair. I was outside the zone of influence and the lack of powers was tangible. I wondered if that feeling would go away after time. If I would get used to not having my power and not being in Carterville.

Powers, just like people, aren't all one thing, not all good, not all bad. Take Patty, what must it be like always knowing what people want from you? Or Smitty, healing is hard on him and was turning him prematurely grey. Or even Frank, his ability to commune with plants has made it harder for him to be around people. And Annie, people came to her when they were so desperate for unconsciousness.

Powers aren't all one thing, especially mine.

And then it hit me. If Smitty had figured out what my power was... well, that explained everything. Well, not everything, but it gave us our missing motive if not whose power was used.

I got my cell phone out and dialed Ortega, put it on speaker mode and put the truck in gear.

"Hey, Boss, what's up?" she said, a bit of surprise in her voice.

"Where are you?" Not a very good greeting, but I was excited.

"Flagstaff. Shopping day, you know."

"Good," I said. "Stay there tonight. Get a hotel if you need to. I'll foot the bill."

"Wait. What…? Why?" she asked.

I wasn't making much sense, talking too fast. "I've got motive," I said. "It was Smitty. It's—"

"Smitty?" she asked, cutting me off. "Why would he want to hurt Frank Paulson?"

"That's the whole thing. He didn't care about hurting Frank, he wants to get me out of town. He hurt Frank so I would agree to leave town if he healed him. He knew I'd do anything for Frank. Simple as that. It was right there all along."

"But whose power was used on Malcom Bishop?" she asked.

I shrugged. "That's what I need you to help with. I want you to find a judge in the morning. We need a warrant to look at Smitty's phone records. This had to be coordinated to happen when Bo was in town—so if we started looking at powers, we would look at him. While I was at the diner. While Frank was cooking. I'm guessing he's arrogant enough to not use a burner phone for his little conspiracy."

There was silence on the other end, but I heard her taking some deep breaths. "Screw the judge, Boss," she said, her voice suddenly forceful. "We need to stop whoever has the power to

do this. And now. I know somebody. She owes me and she…
well… It won't be legal, but I—"

I didn't hesitate, desperate times and all that. "Do it. I'll
take the heat, just do it. We can go the legal route if we
need to."

"Got it," she said, her voice excited. "I'll need an hour
or so."

An hour or so, that meant that she knew what this person
was doing. Did "by the book" Ortega have a hacker girlfriend
in Flagstaff?

I nodded my head. "Good." I paused for a moment, my
mind turning this over and I felt my power return to me as I
got within five miles of Carterville. "Do me a favor, though,
and stay in Flag tonight. Okay?"

"Why?" she asked, her voice tentative, a bit childlike.

"Just do it, okay. Promise me, Isabella." I never used her
first name unless I was damn serious.

"Yeah… yeah…," she said. "I… I promise."

———

HOPE WAS BACK, BUT NOT LIKE LAST NIGHT WITH PATTY. IT WAS
a hope for justice, a hope that Carterville would be better off
without Smitty, provided we could prove what he did. It
wasn't hope for me.

I was leaving whether he did it or not.

I gave my word. I promised.

Just like I knew that Ortega would keep her promise to me
and stay away from Carterville tonight, I knew I would keep
my promise to Smitty.

That is my power, the power of promises made. If I'm involved, if the promise is keepable, it will be kept.

My headlights stabbed out at the thickening darkness as I took the twisty two-lane road through the juniper/piñon forest back to Carterville. Despite the cooling evening, I had the window down and let the cold air blow on me. I needed to be as awake as I could be.

This is why I told the whole town I didn't have a power. Well, at first, I didn't think I had a power, but then I promised some pretty stupid things before I figured out what was happening. Like the time I made a drunken promise to my sister and ended up sledding down the west side of Carterville Hill in my underwear and boots one winter. It was below zero that year and I almost had a heart attack.

If people know about my power, they will try to extract promises from me and won't promise me anything.

Talk about a double-edged power.

But maybe there was a sliver of hope for me too. A life without this power, without promises being so very binding. To be honest, I'm not sure we humans are properly equipped to keep our word like that. Things change, you know.

When I got home, I had purpose and energy and a bit of hope, but that didn't last long.

I paused, gripping the steering wheel, and a chill ran through me like when I was a kid and first went to the Carterville graveyard on a dare with my sister. I was eight and it was around midnight and we had snuck out of the house. When we got there, an owl hooted and we both ran home, jumping at every shadow along the way.

It felt like that, like danger that I could feel but I couldn't see. I grabbed the small revolver I kept under my seat, pushed it into the back of my jeans, and tried to ignore the creepy feeling.

As soon as I stepped out of my truck, my heart fluttered and I felt something… like someone was squeezing my brain, and I felt compelled to go around the side of the house to the deck. My feet moved as if of their own volition.

I hadn't experienced anything like this before, but I knew that this was a Carterville power being used on me. It couldn't be anything else.

I tried to fight, but it was useless. I zombie-shuffled my way to my back deck despite resisting with everything I had.

When I found Patty calmly sitting in the moonlight in one of my Adirondack chairs, my heart broke.

———

PATTY WALSH WAS NOT A CARTERVILLE NATIVE. SHE CAME HERE from Colorado after a bad divorce. In Arizona, even the high country is pretty dry, but we do have the San Francisco Peaks and the huge ponderosa pine forest and it's just the kind of place a Colorado escapee would like. If you like to be outside, Northern Arizona is a great place to live.

But Carterville was just a chance stop. She had come down through the four corners where the states of Colorado, Utah, New Mexico, and Arizona meet and saw the billboard right off Highway 89. "Visit historic Carterville. Tour a Working Silver Mine." It showed a bucolic scene of Main Street with the old brick buildings and the mountain rising behind. She was tired of the desert, tired of the drive, and on a whim took the detour.

Never mind that the sign was twenty years old, badly

faded, and the silver mine had long ago closed to tourists. We had some good rock shops, but that was about it.

This was seven years ago, not long before the meteor hit. Carterville was a sleepy little town struggling economically where not much ever happened.

As fate would have it, I was the first person she talked to. There's a public parking lot down at the bottom of the hill and I was nearby writing a parking ticket on Main Street.

"Excuse me, Officer," she said.

It took me a moment to find my voice. I was two years divorced and seeing Annie Smith at the time, but I'd never seen hair that red or eyes that green. She had on jeans and a tie-dyed T-shirt that highlighted her feminine curves.

"How can I help you, ma'am?" I asked, tipping my cowboy hat to her. Yeah, I know, not regulation, but I was the chief of police, I had been for a while, and I got to wear whatever hat I wanted to wear. Besides, it went well with the western image of our town.

"Is there someplace good to eat around here?" she asked.

I smiled. "Sure is. The Carterville Diner is run by my best friend, Frank Paulson. You'll love him and you'll love the food. Just give me a moment and I'll walk you right up there."

She nodded and smiled and I finished that ticket as fast as I could and kept sneaking glances at Patty. Sure I was with someone, but she was a tourist, she'd be here for an hour or two, and I'd never see her again.

On the walk up Main Street, she told me she was a school-teacher and an artist, that she had taught high school art in Denver. That she was not sure where she was going, but just couldn't stay in Denver anymore. She had a cousin in Phoenix and that was her destination for now.

I was surprised. The uniform generally caused people to keep their mouths shut, but not her. It seemed to do the opposite.

I escorted her to the diner, enjoyed her company, wished her a good day, and was sure I'd never see her again.

When I went into the diner for breakfast the next morning, it was Patty Walsh that took my order. It took me a while to find my tongue.

"I… I thought you were headed to Phoenix," I said when I could finally talk.

She shrugged and smiled sweetly. "Oh, I don't know. This seems like a nice enough place for now. And close enough I can go visit my cousin."

I nodded. "Well, welcome to Carterville," I said, extending my hand. "My name is Henry Carter."

Her hands were a bit rough and her grip strong. "And I'm Patty Walsh. What can I get you for breakfast?"

Patty settled right in, finding a place she could afford, and she liked working at the diner. Said it gave her a lot of time for her painting.

After that, I started going into the diner even more than I did before. We slowly got to know each other and that initial fascination just never really went away.

Soon the meteor hit and everything changed, but I never doubted, for a moment, that Patty wasn't my friend until I zombie-walked my way onto my deck, under the control of someone's power, and saw her sitting there.

———

I'VE OFTEN PONDERED THE EXTENT OF MY POWER. I DO KNOW that for my power to come to bear, the promising party must be in the zone of influence.

So while I had extracted a promise from Ortega, she was not in the zone of influence when she made it, but I knew that if she didn't keep her word, as soon as she got within five miles of Carterville, she would be compelled to leave.

Something similar would happen with my promise to Smitty. Come Wednesday at the time I made the promise, I would be compelled to leave until I exited the zone of influence and then the compulsion would be gone. But if I tried to return, entered the zone of influence again, I would be immediately compelled to leave. If it got bad, if I fought it, I would just bounce off the edge of the zone of influence like a pinball off a bumper.

When I saw Patty sitting in the silvery moonlight on my deck, my mind was very much like a pinball bouncing all over the place.

Patty, who had always been my friend, was behind the attack on Frank, had worked with Smitty to get me to leave my town, had figured out my power and how to use it against me?

I suspected she knew my power. She knew what I wanted, and I had wanted to share it with her, tell it to my friend, many times.

But the rest? I couldn't be that wrong, could I?

And then I saw her eyes. They were wide and she was breathing heavily. She was sitting in the aged Adirondack chair, but her spine was too straight and her arms resting on her lap looked unnatural. She was dressed in sweats like last night, her hair damp, and I saw a shiver run through her.

She was a victim of this power too.

"Patty…?" I asked.

Her nostrils flared and she nodded, tears leaking out of her eyes.

"She can't talk right now." The voice was a bit nasally and arrogant as hell. Smitty. I noticed that my sliding glass door was open and three dark figures stood there just inside. "It's not like we can have her screaming," he added. He chuckled and the sound sent a shiver down my spine. "Well… not until we need her to."

I squinted at the darkness trying to see who flanked the taller Smitty. They were all shadows, but they were shorter than him, one much shorter, and I was pretty sure they were both women.

"Don't do this, Smitty," I said, fighting to move my body which was now hovering menacingly over Patty. "I'm already leaving town. Carterville will be all yours."

He snorted. "Always behind the times, aren't you, Chief? Carterville is *already* all mine."

Powers change you. Mine changed me. I was reluctant to commit to things. Even things far short of a promise. Could be why it took me so long to ask Patty out—I was afraid of the kinds of promises that lovers make to each other and it's not like my time with Annie had been a walk in the park or anything. Smitty's power had changed him—well, he was never a nice guy, but he wasn't a true villain before the powers.

"Stand up, Patty dear," another one of the shadows said. Her voice was aged and much harder than I was used to hearing it. Mary Reilly. The person with the most power closest to me. Someone I trusted.

Patty lurched up, her face contorting as she tried to resist Mary's power.

"Stand nice and still, Chief," Mary continued. "Now Patty, scratch him good on the face so he bleeds."

Patty extended her hand, clawlike, and raked it across my face, sharp pain blossoming in several lines across my check. She whimpered while she did it.

"Why, Mary?" I gasped. "Why?"

"She's just betting on the winner," a third voice said, and my heart sank. It was Annie Smith, and suddenly it all came into focus. I had been so stupid. It hadn't been one power used on Malcom Bishop, but two. Mary had controlled him and Annie had blacked him out. In my defense, I didn't know that Mary's power worked without speaking, like when she took control of me when I got home. No one had known that. Whether it had been that way all along and she just hadn't told anyone, or her powers had changed, I didn't know.

I didn't have time to think about it then, but I suspected the former. Her power was known but it made sense that she had hid the true extent of it.

"I'm sorry, Henry," Annie said, her voice suddenly losing its bravado. "This town just isn't big enough for the two of you."

On the arm of the Adirondack chair Patty had been sitting in was a steak knife from my kitchen. My stomach clenched as Smitty's plan became clear. Mary would force me to hurt Patty and Patty would defend herself. We would both die in the struggle.

It's not like my infatuation with Patty was a secret in a town this small.

When the lurid details came out, my name and my family's

name would be ruined. I wouldn't be surprised if Smitty's town council voted to change the name of the town. And with both of us dead, their secret would be safe.

No, that's not right. Ortega knew my theory. They couldn't be sure of what she knew. Even so, I figured they had something horrible planned for her too.

"Why are you doing this, Mary?" I asked.

I had broken Annie's heart, several times, and our relationship had been more than a little tumultuous. She was no fan of mine, and I could see why she would want me out of town, but to risk Frank like they did, to participate in this now? I couldn't see it. Even more so for kind, old Mary Reilly.

Mary snorted. "William is dead because of you." The words were ice cold, the age in Mary's voice turning into a predatorial growl. She had such power, but she had been powerless to save her husband. She blamed me.

"And she needs me," Smitty said with a smile in his voice.

And then something else I hadn't seen clicked into place. "The Alzheimer's," I said. It wasn't a question.

"Sweet how you all thought it was her powers or Carterville itself keeping it at bay," he said. "No, it is me. My power. Every week. That damn disease just won't quite go away."

I knew this about Smitty's power. Things like fixing Frank after he was stabbed was permanent. Degenerative issues required continued treatment and staying in Carterville. So without Smitty, Mary will have the horrible death of Alzheimer's.

But more than that, anyone who saw Smitty regularly became addicted to his power and how it made you feel. Mary was addicted to Smitty's power, so of course she blamed me for the fiasco that occurred when William had his heart attack and not Smitty. Add on to the grief and addiction how a power as potent as Mary's can change you and it wasn't really a surprise that the kindly grandmother had gone bad. It's why I had kept her close since we understood what her power was.

With Smitty's ability to addict people to his power on top of the superpower of healing, was it any wonder that he had this town wrapped around his finger? How many people would do anything he asked to stay healthy, to feed their addiction?

"And what does he have on you, Annie?" I asked.

"Enough!" Smitty snapped. "Let's get this over with."

Patty whimpered again and it broke my heart to see her this way, shaking and struggling and knowing what was coming but being powerless to change it.

We were both powerless.

Wait. Powers. My power.

"How did you know about my power?" I asked, mostly stalling for time. I needed to think.

"That was me," Annie said quietly. "You don't sleep with a man and not get to know him and his secrets."

I changed after the meteor. We all did. Once I understood my power, it changed how I talked to people, how I interacted with them, always being careful to stay away from promises. Annie saw those changes and she put it together.

"Listen," I whispered to Patty, hoping it was low enough so the others couldn't hear. "I promise you that—"

"No, no," Mary growled. "That's enough talking from you, Chief. Now is not the time for promises you can't keep." My jaw snapped shut hard enough to rattle my teeth.

But I forged on, mumbling, "—I will get us out of this."

I didn't know if Patty could hear it. I didn't know if it was enough. But it was all I had. My power against Mary's powers. The power of promises versus the power of control.

My arms rose in front of me of their own volition, my hands stretched out at the level of Patty's throat. I took a halting step and looked like nothing other than a zombie.

"Wait…" Annie gasped and I suddenly stopped moving. "Let me… let me knock them out."

There was silence for a moment, and I started muttering my promise under my breath. "I promise you, Patty, I will get us out of this. I promise you, Patty, that I will get us out of this."

"Fine," Smitty hissed. "Knock her out, but not him."

He didn't say anything else, but it was implied. He wanted me to suffer. For being a policeman, for doing my job, for arresting him when he was just human, for standing in his way when he was a villain, for choosing to save him last during the "Destroyer" mess when I had to make all those hard choices, for all those reasons he wanted me to suffer before I died.

"I promise that I will get us out of this," I mumbled as I watched Patty's eyes unfocus and her face relax. "I will stop them, I promise."

And I understood what had happened with Annie. Bitterness can erode your soul and after our final breakup, after I seriously considered her in the Lila Chang murder case, she had come to truly hate me. She had agreed to a plan to use my powers against me and get me out of Carterville, even to hurt Frank to do it, but hadn't expected it to come to this, to come to murder. Now she was in too deep to stop. She had made a deal with the wrong man.

When she explained Mary's actions by saying she was

betting on the winner, she was talking about herself. She saw that Smitty was going to win, eventually, and wanted to be on the right side of things when it finally happened.

I kept mumbling, pleading to my powers, but I didn't really believe it would be enough. Not when I stumbled forward another step and my hands wrapped around Patty's throat. Not when I started to squeeze. Not when I felt her racing heartbeat against my hand.

But I kept promising and promising and promising. It was the only thing I could do. It was the only thing that I had. I was a Carter. I was a policeman. I was a man of my word.

So I gave it to Patty hoping it would be enough.

————

Back in Flagstaff, Isabella Ortega had no intentions of keeping her word when she hung up the phone after talking to me. She knew me well. Not my power, she swears she had no idea what my power was, but it was completely obvious that I was trying to protect her. That I was scared. That I was alone. That Smitty was dangerous.

She dropped her purchases, ran out of the Wal-Mart, and got in her 1998 Ford Mustang. Being young she was good at all that voice command stuff and started making phone calls while she drove. Way too fast, I might add.

She called her hacker friend and had her start trying to get Smitty's phone records.

And then she called the most powerful person she knew in Carterville, one who could help me if things went south, one who was like family, one who worked with us regularly. Mary Reilly.

Now, I don't blame her. There was nothing wrong with her thought process. Neither of us could conceive of Mary being a part of this. So Ortega called her, told her we were quite sure Smitty was behind it and that she should get to my house and make sure I was okay.

"Don't you worry yourself a bit, Isabella," Mary told her. "I'll make sure our chief is just fine."

By then she was on I-40, the Mustang surging forward, dancing from lane to lane, gambling she wouldn't be pulled over, and if she was, she could flash her badge and talk her way out of it.

Her next call was to Annabelle Unger, another team member, another person we trusted. Annabelle is way more on the quirky end of the power spectrum. She can levitate things, but only small things and only briefly. She had pushed herself far past that once to save my life, and it had cost her, but that's not why Ortega called her. She was calling her for moral support.

Annabelle listened to the update and then got quiet on the other end of the line.

"What?" Ortega asked when the silence had gone on too long.

"Umm… It's just that… I don't know," Annabelle said.

"Come on, just tell me."

"Well… Mary has been a bit off lately. She don't come to book club anymore. She's broken a couple coffee dates with me. She… I don't know, I'm just probably spooked by this whole damn thing."

Ortega mulled it over in that fine mind of hers and said, "I'm sure it's fine, Annabelle. Don't you worry."

When she hung up, she pressed the pedal farther down

and made one more call. To one more person who just might have enough power to counteract Mary if there was an issue. Another person we trusted and felt like family, and another person on our list of suspects.

Bo Larson.

In her mind she figured she might be wrong about Mary or she might be wrong about Bo, but there was no way she was wrong about both.

Well, at least she hoped.

She got him on the phone and told him what was going on and he was in his truck and headed to Carterville before their conversation was over.

———

I've thought about this a lot. About Mary and her power and my power. They are so damn similar in that they can result in people doing things they didn't think they could do.

But in Mary's case, they will do things against their will. In my case, my power will amplify their will. That is, of course, if I play fair and the promise made to me is genuine and from the heart.

It's that knife edge we all have to walk with our powers, but Mary's is so much sharper than mine. That combined with her disease and her blaming me for her husband's death drove her to Smitty. To this night. To my hands wrapped around Patty's neck and squeezing.

Patty screamed, but it was a strange halting scream, her eyes still unfocused, Annie's power keeping her under, but Mary's power animating the scream.

Smitty chuckled.

I shook and strained and sweated. I continued to mumble my promise through my locked jaws thinking maybe I didn't have the power, maybe I had to speak it clearly, maybe I hadn't found the right promise.

And then my promises got even more desperate. "I promise not to hurt you, Patty, ever. I will die before I will hurt you."

Things seemed to go silent. I could feel the cool air kicked up by a slight breeze. I could smell my own sweat and Patty's damp hair. I could hear quiet crying from inside my house. That was Annie, not quite as hard hearted as she put on. And most of all I could hear my heartbeat, a fast thump-thump-thump.

But then it went thump-thwonk-thump, almost skipping a beat, my heart slamming into my ribcage and my left arm started to hurt.

My jaw loosened and I gasped at the pain and I felt the pressure in my head, the grip of Mary's power, lessen just a bit.

"I promise not to hurt you, Patty. Ever," I said, my voice weak but it was clear now and my arm hurt even more, my chest constricting and my fingers loosening.

It was working. I had found a promise stronger than Mary's power and I cared not what the cost was.

"I promise not to hurt you, Patty. I..." The pain was mounting, my heart going thwonk more than thump, but I was happy. I was having a heart attack, but I was going to keep my promise to Patty.

I let go of her neck and staggered back. I was suddenly sweating in the cool night. I pulled my gun out of the back of my pants and pointed it towards the shadows standing just inside my house.

"Step… step outside, Mary, and stop using your powers." I could barely speak, the pain was so bad.

"Put him under," Smitty hissed.

"I'm trying," Annie said.

And I could feel Annie's power whispering in my mind, offering me escape and sweet succor. But I ignored it. My power rose up against hers, too. I had made promises and I had to keep them.

"Now, Mary, or I start firing," I said, trying to keep my voice steady, my heart clomping along at a disturbingly irregular pace. "You have to the count of three."

"Go to the edge of the deck, Chief," she growled, taking a small step forward, right to the edge of the door. "Go and jump off. Do it now."

I stumbled back, my legs rebelling against me, but I kept facing Mary. She was still in the house, cloaked in shadow, but because of her height, I was sure which one was her. "One," I said through gritted teeth.

I heard a sharp intake of breath from Patty and she stepped back. Mary and Annie were concentrating their powers on me and Patty was free.

"Step back, Henry," Mary said, her voice rising to a shout. "Now!"

I stumbled back another step, my chest feeling like an elephant was sitting on it. "Two," I said.

To my right, I sensed that Patty was on the move, going around the house the way that I had come in.

Mary stepped out of the house, the moonlight illuminating her silver hair. I heard the sound of a truck on the street outside and then the retreating steps of Smitty and Annie and then a crash and the sound of glass breaking in the house.

"You will jump off this deck, Chief, and you will jump now!" Mary cried.

Her power hit me hard, I wanted to jump off the deck. I needed to jump off the deck. It was clearly the right thing to do, the best thing to do, the only thing to do.

"Three," I grunted and fired the gun, the sharp retort ringing out into the night.

Mary went down.

The pain in my chest blossomed and I went down.

For a moment it was good. I could see the stars above me, the stars as seen from my beloved Carterville. And then Patty was there holding me and it was even better. And then I knew nothing.

———

I DIED THAT NIGHT ON MY DECK IN CARTERVILLE. I SWEAR I did. No one agrees with me, they say what happened next proves I wasn't dead, but I know different.

I was gazing up at the dark night at the shadows of Patty's face, the tumble of her still damp hair, and then the pain was gone. The fire in my chest was no longer there, the pain in my arm disappeared, I was no longer gasping for breath.

But I didn't really have a chest or arms. I wasn't breathing. I was a presence and then I was floating above the deck, floating high above my beloved town, the lights of the houses and the few cars on the street gently illuminating the old buildings and the surrounding trees.

I floated even higher, so high, and saw headlights turning off 89 onto the road to Carterville. A car going much too fast. I knew it was Ortega and I watched in fascination as she hit the zone of influence and kept going.

That's how I knew I was dead. Ortega wasn't keeping her promise. My power wasn't making her because I wasn't alive.

I looked at the graceful mountain with its two high peaks and the scoop out of the inner basin in between. And then I looked down at Carterville. A small town on a small hill in the shadow of a large mountain on the edge of a vast desert.

It wasn't much, just roads and buildings and people. My people. And then I saw the glow.

Well, "saw" is really the wrong word. This was something you couldn't see, but far below my town, deep in a mine shaft underneath sat the glow. The meteor. The source of our powers. The mystery at the center of our lives.

I wanted to go there, to go to the source of the power, to find out what it really was. I felt something, a vague sense of it, and it wasn't a meteor. Or it wasn't *just* a meteor. It was power and awareness and purpose. It was mystery.

As I contemplated this, time passed. I was aware of it passing, but not how much or how fast.

Soon I was floating back down towards my deck, the lights were on and it seemed so bright. At first, I was disappointed. I wanted to go to the mystery, not towards the people, but something caught my attention.

There was a body splayed out on the deck, a middle-aged man with a large belly and thinning brown hair dressed in jeans and a flannel shirt. I was vaguely aware that I was looking at myself.

Another man, thin and angular, was kneeling over that

man, over me. The thin man had blond hair shot with grey and flowing clothing. Smitty. Behind him stood Ortega, her gun out and pointed at him.

Patty was there, hovering over Annie who was sitting awkwardly on the deck, her hands cuffed behind her. Patty looked mad, her fists clenched. Bo Larson was there too, his eyes closed as he breathed deeply. I sent calm thoughts to him, to help him control his anger. Because he was angry and I knew that could be a bad thing.

Mary Reilly was laid out on the deck in a growing pool of blood. She was dead. The big-bellied man had killed her. I had killed her.

I felt this warmth grow around me, like the essence of a spring day, like the power of life itself, and I felt peace, such peace. I had felt this feeling before and it was the best feeling in the world, and I knew I could never get enough of it. The warmth was coming from the angular man, from Smitty. It was so nice.

And then I wasn't hovering anymore and I was slammed into my body and I sucked in a desperate breath. I felt like hell. Like an elephant stampede had just run me over. I sucked in breath after breath into lungs that seemed to have forgotten how to work.

I could feel my heart beating in my chest, a normal thump-thump and I was more exhausted than I had ever been. Warm hands were on my chest, the same as I had felt before.

I opened my eyes and looked up into the green eyes of Winston "Smitty" Smith. One of Smitty's eyes was purple and swelling shut. This pleased me. But I hurt so much that I couldn't possibly be dead anymore. I had to wonder if Smitty's powers had changed or had I been right on that edge between life and death when I floated above my home and my town.

I looked past Smitty and saw Ortega there, her face scrunched like a kid that had waited too long to go to the bathroom. She stepped forward so I could see her clearly. "Umm… I… I'm sorry, Boss. I promised to not come back and then I did. I… I better go now."

Smitty was staring at her, his eyes narrow. I was alive, but weak as a kitten and still coming back to myself. If Ortega left, Smitty would run.

It hurt to think. I wanted to go back up into the sky, I wanted to dive down into the mine and see what that glow was. I wanted to feel free and light, floating under the stars.

But I was a Carter and this was my town.

"I release you from your promise, Ortega," I said, my voice sounding foreign in my ears.

Her face relaxed and she let out a big sigh and smiled.

"Now arrest these people," I said.

Her smile widened. "With pleasure, Boss. With pleasure."

FIVE
TUESDAY

THERE WAS NO WAY I COULD BE READY TO GO IN THE WEEK Smitty and my promise had allotted. Sure, Smitty had saved me from my heart attack, but he had healed me just enough so I would survive, not enough that I could dance a jig or anything.

This was the way it always was with him. This time, I'm sure he did it this way because he didn't want to heal me, and only healed me as much as he did because Ortega had a gun on him. But before, when it had happened, he had done it because he wanted me to come back for more. He wanted to addict me to his power.

And I wanted more. You couldn't feel his healing super-power and not want more. It was like touching the divine, which seemed ironic considering the package it came in.

But I'm old enough to know that that is the way it often is with humanity. If there is anything divine or graceful or transcendent in this world, it has no choice but to express through us flawed humans.

I won't bore you with the details of dealing with the paperwork or the packing and all the many goodbyes save a few.

Monday and Tuesday were a blur of all of that, but I would be remiss if I didn't tell you about Officer Ortega who was about to become acting chief of police.

"Hey, Boss," she said shyly. She had walked around the side of my house to the deck and was wearing jeans and a dark T-shirt. The T-shirt was of a band I did not recognize that played music I would surely not understand, and it just made me feel old.

I was sitting in an Adirondack chair, a drink in my hand, looking at the lengthening shadows out in the desert. I had given up on packing, there just wasn't time, and if I needed more things it was going to fall to my sister.

I smiled and gestured to the Adirondack chair next to mine. There was a cooler between the two chairs with her favorite beer, a local microbrew, iced and ready to go. She hated gin and I had been expecting her.

She sat down and said, "You lied to everybody."

I almost sighed. She was getting right to it, and I knew what she really meant was, "You lied to me."

She had a point. I had told everyone that I didn't have a power when I did. Trust was important, especially in my job, and I had done something quite untrustworthy and I'm sure she, and everyone else, was wondering what else I lied about.

"Yes, I did," I said. "I'm sure you can see why."

She popped a beer, took a long drink, and then nodded. "I would have kept your secret," she said.

"I know," I said, and I did. That was the kind of person she was. "But it would have changed things and I liked the way things were between us."

She nodded again but didn't say anything and turned towards the desert to watch the sunset show which was fine with me.

Often in life we aren't aware of endings when they happen, but that night I knew this might be the last time I would watch the sunset over the desert I loved so much from my deck in Carterville.

When her beer was gone and she was on her second, she said, "This is about 'Destroyer' right? The reason you are leaving so easily?"

I sure as hell wouldn't categorize the last week as "easy" or my experience of this change as anything approaching "easy," but I let it go. I got her point.

I've mentioned the "Destroyer of Carterville" mess here a few times. It's a hell of a story, one I'm guessing I'm going to need to tell, so I won't go into details or give anything away.

It was the kind of thing that can really mess with you, so after it happened, I put it out of my mind because I couldn't function properly if I was always thinking about it. I had ordered Ortega and Annabelle to never mention it, but I wasn't her boss anymore, was I?

I will say that what happened there informed what was happening now in a big way. You could say that what was promised there was coming to pass now.

"Yes," I said.

"Thought so," she said. There was something in her tone, something dismissive.

"You think I can fight it?" I asked.

She shrugged. "Just surprised you are not."

And I wasn't. How could I? The power of my promise would keep me away. I guess I could cross into the zone of influence, but given my promise to leave Carterville, I could never enter the city limits. My power wouldn't let me. If there was a way out of this, I couldn't think of it. Well… if I'm being honest, I didn't seem to be able to even think about it.

Maybe it was my power driving me away. Maybe it was something about having my hands wrapped around Patty's neck. I know Mary made me do it, but that didn't erase the experience. Maybe I had been in this job too damn long and had just barely held this town together with all these powers too many times.

"You're right," I said. "And I'm sorry about the position that puts you in."

She looked at me and those brown eyes of hers looked extra soulful. "I need you to come back, Chief," she said.

I sighed. "Best call me Henry now," I said. "I'm not the chief for much longer."

She shook her head. She only did it twice, but it was a clear and unequivocal refusal.

"I'm sorry, Isabella," I said. "I can't make any promises. I need…" I trailed off because I didn't really know what I needed. A vacation? God, yes. But beyond that, I just didn't know. There had been too much going on for too long for me to even have a clue.

Annie and I were long over, and she was facing serious consequences for her actions. Smitty would be leaving soon as he faced his crimes. Clearly, this was the end of an era, and I didn't know where I fit in.

"I'll be a phone call away," I said. "You call if I can do something from a distance."

"Appreciate it," she said. "But I need you to find a way back."

I nodded, not in agreement but in acknowledgment. There was a lot to consider and there was the whole "Destroyer" thing. Smitty and I had both been called "Destroyer of Carterville" and I was tired enough, beaten down enough to wonder if that was right, to wonder if this town wouldn't be better off without us.

I certainly believed that the town would be better without Smitty. His superpower, while it saved lives, was a corrosive, caustic influence. And I had just started to wonder if Carterville would be better off without me.

We drank and talked late into the night, but I won't share any of that in detail. She needed to talk through what happened on Sunday night on this deck and how she had called Mary first. I couldn't take away her guilt, but I did the best I could and tried to make it clear that I knew she had done the best she could given what we knew. It was a good thing we had plenty of beer and gin.

After that it got easier, lighter, and we talked about town gossip or details about the job, things like that. But to me, it was bittersweet. Officer Isabella Ortega was feeling more and more like a daughter, and she was going to be hard to leave.

Hell, let's face it. Even with all my doubts, with all that had happened in the last few years, Carterville, and everyone in it, was going to be hard to leave.

SIX
WEDNESDAY

"So, you are really leaving," Frank said.

I looked up from my truck. I had been loading big plastic tubs with my camping gear into the badly scratched bed. The pickup truck, like me, had seen a lot of life, but it could still move when it needed to.

I was glad to see him for so many reasons. He was my best friend and I was happy he was alive. The promise I made to get him healed was the reason I was leaving, and it was only right that we talked. And it gave my mind something else to do besides reliving those images of my hands squeezing Patty's throat.

I had not been sleeping well, and while I understood that Mary Reilly made me do it with her powers, it didn't change how it felt. I had the pain of the three deep scratches on my cheek that was a constant reminder of what we did under the influence of Mary's power.

The morning had snapped cold and we both had jackets

on. In a few weeks, the aspens would start turning up in the inner basin. Fall is the most beautiful time around here and I hated to leave, but I had to. I promised.

I nodded and smiled. Frank had walked up here and I could see the strain in his face, but that was just the normal strain of an overweight, middle-aged man getting the exercise he needed. He had gotten home yesterday and I hadn't seen him yet. There had been a lot of paperwork to do for the case which had kept Ortega and me very busy.

"Is… is it this power of yours?" he asked, taking a few steps until we were about six feet apart. We both stood there awkwardly, our hands shoved into our jean pockets.

He pulled a thin newspaper out of his back pocket, a recent copy of our local newspaper, *The Carterville Silver Star*, that I had studiosly been avoiding. He waved it nervously and said, "The whole town is talking. They're calling you the Promise Keeper."

My stomach tightened even though all I had this morning was a couple of sips of coffee. I nodded to the house and said, "Not here."

We walked around the side and out onto the deck. The blood stain of where Mary fell was still there. The deck would need to be sanded and re-stained to get it out. Even then I would always know and I would always hate what I had done.

The fact that I was defending myself and my town, that my actions, while they were still under review, were justified, doesn't change the fact that I killed someone I had known my entire life. Well… someone I hadn't really known as well as I had thought.

As I've thought about it, I've come to a conclusion. I don't really blame Mary for what she became. It was the power granted to her and the disease that befell her and the accident and poor timing of her husband's death.

I'm not sure what I would have become under the same circumstances.

Now, this does not excuse her crimes, it's just how I have to look at it in my mind. I need to remember the kind Mary Reilly from before everything changed.

Frank caught me staring at the stain but didn't say a word. He took my arm and gently guided me to the edge of the deck, the early morning light making the desert colors deeper and darker than normal, the painted desert looking even more like a painting.

"The internet seems to have found us again. The paper says they're calling Annie 'Blackout' and Mary 'Puppet Master,'" Frank said quietly. "Our little town is about to get a whole lot busier. And what is this with the names now? Like we're in some goddamn stupid movie."

I shrugged and just tried to soak in the view I was about to leave.

"I promised Smitty," I finally said after we had stood there for a few minutes. "So, yes, I have to keep that promise."

"And when he leaves?" Frank asked gently. "I hear others have been coming forward, telling what he did to them."

I nodded. "We've been taking statements for the last two days. I've spoken with the Coconino County attorney and there is more than enough to make a case against him, even with the powers involved and how tricky that can get, but…"

"But what?" Frank asked.

I sighed. "Smitty can heal people. He saved your life. He saved my life. That… that is a powerful thing."

Frank grabbed me by the shoulder and yanked me around

until I was looking into his cool blue eyes. "You're not thinking of letting him go, are you?"

"God, no! I want to see him go to prison for a long time. But look what he did to Mary. Look how he has already changed this town. How many promises do you think he'll have to make to weasel himself back here?"

Frank's nostrils flared and he slowly nodded, his eyes darkening and flicking away from mine.

"How many people, right now, are blaming me for Mary's death?" I asked. "She was well loved. I think it's for the best that I leave."

Just because we don't like the way the world works, it doesn't mean that it really isn't that way.

We were silent again for a few minutes watching the sun rise and the desert slowly lighten. "You're the reason I stopped smoking, aren't you?" Frank finally asked.

I nodded. "Lisa was threatening to leave you and you had failed three times before."

"And you made me promise you and I suddenly had the willpower I had lacked before."

I nodded.

"What happens when you leave?" he asked, a bit of fear in his voice. "Will I start smoking again?"

I shook my head. "Not while you are in Carterville, and not unless I release you from your promise. And I'm not going to do that."

"And that means you can't come back here unless Smitty releases you from your promise," Frank said. He was finally getting it.

"Right," I said. "If the promise is made to or by me, Carterville will make sure the promise is kept. And it's not like

Smitty is going to release me from my promise."

"I can't believe you never told me," he said, his voice low.

"I never told anyone, Frank. Don't you see? How can I do my job, how can I live my life when people are thinking of me as 'Promise Keeper'?"

There was another span of silence. "But you are a Carter," he said. "This town needs you."

He didn't make it personal. He didn't say that he needed me, and for that, I was grateful.

I didn't answer his assertion. I couldn't. We stood there and chatted a bit about other town news, safe topics. And then he helped me finish packing the truck and I drove him down to the diner. It wasn't open yet but he talked me into coming in so he could make me breakfast before I hit the road.

Patty was there sitting on a stool at the counter, my usual spot, and she spun around and gave me a look when we walked in. Her face was slack, neutral, but her eyes were hard.

Frank excused himself and Patty slowly rose, her arms crossed and her lips a thin line. She was wearing old ripped jeans and a grey Mickey Mouse sweatshirt. Her red hair was pulled back and she wasn't wearing any makeup.

Around her neck was a black scarf hiding the marks my hands had made there.

"Henry Carter," she said quietly. "Were you going to leave town and not say goodbye to me?"

My mouth was dry and my heart was beating so loudly in my ears that for a moment I worried that I was having another heart attack. That Smitty hadn't really healed me properly.

I promised to never hurt her, but how was that a promise I

could keep? We were friends and if I left without seeing her, that would be hurtful, but if I did see her, how could that not hurt?

I was stuck in a promise I couldn't keep. My mouth moved, but I couldn't find any words yet. I studied her lovely face and those green eyes showed the same kind of pain I saw when I looked into the mirror.

"Henry," she began, swallowing hard. "I release you from your promise to never hurt me. I release you from every promise you've ever made to me."

I felt a wave of energy pass through me and I sighed, my shoulders slumping in relief as if I had just been relieved of a great burden. Patty was there when I released Ortega from her promise. She knew how my powers worked and I was grateful.

"Patty, I'm so sorry that I…" the words started with a rush and then just faltered. To say it would make it more real, and it was far too real already.

"It wasn't you," she said, but she still stood there with her arms wrapped around her chest.

I heard the sound of bacon sizzling from the back and wished that this was just breakfast. I wasn't the least bit hungry now.

I slowly nodded. "I know it wasn't me, but…" I took a deep breath. "It feels like it was me."

Her eyes teared up and she nodded. "I know. I'm sorry about your face." She started to reach out with her hand as if she wanted to touch my injured cheek, but her hand fell quickly to her side.

I shrugged. It still hurt and I was pretty sure I was going to be left with a scar, but I didn't care about it.

"I didn't see this coming," she began, her eyes darkening and her nostrils flaring. "I mean, I knew Smitty wanted you gone, the whole town knew that. But Mary… I should have seen that. My powers…. I should have known." She ended with a sigh and looking like any fight she had had drained out.

"I should have seen it too. Don't blame yourself, Patty… please."

She gave me a wry smile. "And don't you blame yourself, Henry."

But we both knew it wasn't that simple. Seconds ticked by and the silence became awkward.

"I'm… I'm going back to Colorado," she finally said. "I am going to stay with my sister for a while. She knows a good therapist, so I'm… I'm going to do that."

I stood there, my jaw moving, but I couldn't speak. I was the one that was going to leave town. I was the one that would pay the price for all of this.

But that was just my damn ego talking. Everyone had to deal with this in their own way. I couldn't fix this for her, and I had no idea how to fix this for myself.

"You should find someone to talk to," she said.

I nodded and then she was gone. She walked carefully around me and walked away without a glance back. I went to the window and watched her walk up Main Street, her spine erect, her pace quick. It seemed clear that she wasn't coming back.

She was just a pawn in Smitty's scheme to get rid of me.

I stood there until I heard Frank clear his throat. He was at the counter, two steaming breakfasts ready to eat.

I walked over and slumped onto the stool, still warm from when Patty had been sitting there.

"So, is Ortega okay?" Frank asked.

I nodded absently and poked at the sunny-side-up eggs. "She feels so guilty for calling Mary, for letting them know how much we knew and catalyzing what happened on my deck, but…" I shrugged. "She also called Bo Larson, and if she hadn't, Smitty and Annie would have run and I would have died. So there's that. She's dealing with it."

The smell of the bacon and eggs and toast got to me and suddenly I was voraciously hungry. We ate silently and quickly.

Frank hugged me fiercely before I left and told me that he loved me. I told it to him right back even though the two of us have never said those words to each other before.

He held me at arm's length, his eyes moist. "Will you come back?" The question was bare, unadorned, and asked plainly. It didn't carry expectation with it, Frank was just that kind of guy. He just wanted to know.

I swallowed and shook my head. "I don't know, Frank. I can't make any promises."

He smiled and nodded. "Well… I sure as hell better hear from you."

"I promise," I said, quietly.

Frank rolled his eyes and chuckled. "Get out of here, old man. I've got a business to attend to."

———

BY THE TIME I LEFT FRANK, IT WAS LIKE I HAD ANTS IN MY pants. I was restless and twitchy and desperate to get away.

My power and my promise were coming to bear. Smitty saved Frank and I had to leave town. There was no choice. At least not while Smitty held me to my promise.

If not for my power, I wouldn't have left. This was my town, bore my name, and all my roots were here. And there were the many people I was leaving, Isabella Ortega foremost on my mind.

Just because I was gone, just because Smitty would soon be gone, didn't suddenly make this an easy place to be a cop. There were still 196 people left with powers.

"I'm a phone call away," I had told her when we said our goodbyes on Tuesday.

It seemed like the mountain was finally done with me, maybe it was even done with us Carters. Without me there, I suspected my sister wouldn't be spending much time in Carterville. It was a sad thought, but all things must end.

As I drove down the twisting two-lane road, I rolled the window down and let the cool September air blow on my face. It felt like winter was coming early and like it was going to be a long one.

When I got past the edge of the zone of influence and the low-level hum of my power disappeared, I breathed a sigh of relief and pulled over and smelled the sharp scent of the junipers. The restlessness was gone, but I was left with something I wasn't used to. The unknown. My future wasn't clear anymore. It seemed the mountain was done with me, at least for now, and that meant that I didn't have a home. I didn't have a purpose.

All I had was a truck full of camping gear and a cooler full of food. I didn't have Carterville to take care of, only myself.

I looked back, but of course I couldn't see Carter Hill, it

was lost in the folds of forested land. But I could feel it, the powers and the troubles that I was leaving behind.

Patty was right, I probably need to see a therapist, find someone to help me sort through all of this. But for now, I was going to drive around to the North Rim of the Grand Canyon, navigate the old forest service roads, and find a place to camp where I could see a bit of the canyon and be away from people and powers and responsibility.

The stars and the campfire and the Grand Canyon would be my therapy for now.

I hated leaving Carterville, the town that bore my name, and yet I was also glad to leave. It had been too much for too long, a constant rush of emergencies since the meteor hit. I pushed away the forever nature of my leaving, I couldn't go there yet, I couldn't imagine never returning, and focused on taking a well-earned break.

I took a deep breath and let out a long sigh. I needed a rest. I needed a break. And God knows, I needed a good night's sleep.

I smiled and pulled back onto the road. The future wasn't clear for me anymore and right then that seemed just about perfect.

.

WANT MORE CARTERVILLE?

Carterville is all about possibilities. A picturesque mountain town filled with people with powers. Mystery. Romance. Adventure. It is a ripe environment for these kinds of stories. A place where nearly anything can happen.

When the idea came to me (a hat tip to Stephen King and his fictional town in Maine, Castle Rock) I knew I was onto something. I love my Arizona mountain home. Much of the southwest was founded on mining and I have loved exploring these places. Where history and tradition collide with the modern world (and mix in powers with Carterville) there are fascinating stories.

If you'd like more adventures in Carterville, let me know. Post a review of this book, reach out to me through my website RobertJMcCarter.com, or on facebook (@RobertJMc-CarterAuthor) or twitter (@RobertJMcCarter). Let me know what kind of Carterville stories you'd like to see.

The best way to find out when things happen in Carterville is to sign up for my email newsletter at RobertJMc-Carter.com/newsletter. When you subscribe you'll get a free 750+ page ebook, *Bits, Bites, and Rarities: The Worlds of Robert J. McCarter*, that introduces you to my many series, and has four stories you can't read anywhere else!

Or, if you'd like a different kind of mystery, check out my *Walter Anchor, Ghost Detective* series. That's right. A ghost who solves murders. The ebook of the first case, *Detecting Haley*, is free when you sign up for my newsletter. Read on to learn more about this story.

Detecting Haley

A Ghost Trying to Solve His Own Murder...

Walter Anchor hates being a ghost. He wants nothing more than to solve his own murder, finish his unfinished business as an earthbound spirit, and "move on." But when he and his best ghost-friend Emily stumble across a corpse while tracking clues to his murder, everything changes.

The dead girl used to work for Walter and he hopes

solving her murder will lead to his own killer. But the case gets complicated and things get personal. Walter finds himself dealing with a much bigger problem than solving his own murder.

From the author of *Shuffled Off: A Ghost's Memoir* comes a murder mystery unlike anything seen before.

Get a copy today, or free when you sign up for my newsletter.

ABOUT THE AUTHOR

Robert J. McCarter is the author of more than ten novels and over a hundred short stories. He is a regular contributor to *Pulphouse Fiction Magazine* and his short fiction has also appeared in *The Saturday Evening Post, Andromeda Spaceways Inflight Magazine, Everyday Fiction,* and numerous anthologies.

Robert writes in a variety of genres from contemporary fantasy to science fiction and just about everything in between. His diverse background—including a career in software engineering, growing up on a ranch riding horses, and acting—colors the stories he tells.

He lives in the mountains of Arizona with his amazing wife and his ridiculously adorable dogs.

Find out more at:
RobertJMcCarter.com

BOOKS BY ROBERT J. MCCARTER

Carterville Mysteries

- **Out of a Christmas Sky**
- **Destroyer of Carterville**
- **The Blood of Carterville**

Walter Anchor, Ghost Detective Stories

- **Case 1: Detecting Haley** (also part of *Life After: Stories of Life, Death, and the Places in Between*)
- **Case 2: The Ghost Bride's Gift**
- **Case 3: A Long Hard Fall**
- **Case 4: Death of a Dentist**
- **Case 5: A Hollywood Kind of a Murder**
- **Case 6: The Red Arrow Murders**
- **Unfinished Business: The Cases of Walter Anchor Ghost Detective**

For a complete list of Walter Anchor stories, go to RobertJMcCarter.com/WalterAnchor

Novels in the "Ghost's Memoir" world:

- Shuffled Off: A Ghost's Memoir, Book 1
- Drawing the Dead

- To Be a Fool: A Ghost's Memoir, Book 2
- Of Things Not Seen: A Ghost's Memoir, Book 3
- A Boy, a Girl, and a Ghost

For a complete list the "Ghost's Memoir" novels, go to ShuffledOff.com

The Woody and June versus the Apocalypse Series

Find out more at WoodyAndJune.com

The Neutrinoman and Lightningirl Series

Find out more at Neutrinoman.com

Other Novels:

- Seeing Forever
- Where the Past Belongs: An Angelica and Ash Time Travel Adventure

For a more information, go to RobertJMcCarter.com